To Alex, who is exceptional.

TRIAL BY MAGIC

DRAGON'S GIFT THE PROTECTOR BOOK 2

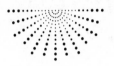

LINSEY HALL

ACKNOWLEDGMENTS

Thank you, Ben, for everything. There would be no books without you.

Thank you to Lindsey Loucks for your excellent editing. The book is immensely better because of you! Thank you to Crystal Jeffs, for your help making the story better. Thank you to Jessi Crosby for your keen eyes. Thank you to Sapna Moriani Bhog for suggesting the Rann of Kutch in Rajasthan in India as a location for a scene in the book, and to Sarah Keyes for suggesting the burning bridge. Thank you Katrina N. Berry for suggesting adobe as the material for Nix's bridge. Thank you to Rebecca Frank for the cover art and to Orina Kafe for the cover edits.

The Dragon's Gift series is a product of my two lives: one as an archaeologist and one as a novelist. Combining these two took a bit of work. I'd like to thank my friends, Wayne Lusardi, the State Maritime Archaeologist for Michigan, and Douglas Inglis and Veronica Morris, both archaeologists for Interactive Heritage, for their ideas about how to have a treasure hunter heroine that doesn't conflict too much with archaeology's ethics. The Author's Note contains a bit more about this if you are interested.

CHAPTER ONE

"How much farther?" I wheezed as I raced alongside Cass, my *deirfiúr*. We were sisters by choice and partners in all things deadly. Today's task was returning an ancient artifact to a tomb in northern England.

"Almost there, Nix." Cass pointed to the top of the steep hill we were climbing. "Just over the hill, I think."

"Hill?" My lungs burned. "Mini mountain, more like."

Cass laughed and picked up the pace, sprinting over the rocky moorland. Muted sunlight illuminated the mist covering the ground.

I raced to catch up.

We were in the Yorkshire Dales, which was really too benign a name for such a bleak and deadly place. The landscape was punctuated by peaks that fell off into cliffs and valleys. Chill wind whipped my hair back from my face. Black clouds rolled over the horizon, chasing us as we searched for the archaeological site where Cass had found the clay vase that sat safely in my backpack.

Technically, it was called a beaker from the Bronze Age Bell Beaker Culture, but it was really just a vase. Ugly but very magical. Last week, some demons had tried to steal it from our shop. Fortunately, I'd gotten it back from the thieves.

As if they'd stood a chance against me.

"I seriously need to get out more." I wheezed as I leapt over a boulder stuck into the scrubby ground. This run was killing me. Too much time behind the shop counter. I could kick ass if someone tried to rob us, but a run was not in my skillset.

"Nearly there." Cass's breath was heaving, too.

I grinned. Good.

Normally, she'd be able to transport us to where we wanted to go, but the weird magic that haunted the dales made it difficult to end up in the right place. And because this area was known for sinkholes...

Not a good idea to appear out of thin air.

We crested the huge hill, and Cass halted abruptly. I followed suit, skidding on the ground.

Ahead of us, one of the famous sinkholes plunged deep into the earth.

"Whoa." I surveyed the giant hole. "We're really going in that?"

"Yep." Cass crept up to the edge.

My heart thundered as I followed, sweat breaking out on my skin. The cool breeze chilled it. I shivered.

"If we want to return that beaker, we're going in," Cass said. "Once we go down the sinkhole, there are tunnels leading to chambers. I found it in a tomb at the end of one."

"Of course you did." Ancient artifacts containing valuable magic never hung out in safe, convenient places.

Compared to us, Indiana Jones had it easy.

Cass hunted the artifacts we sold in our shop, Ancient Magic. I ran the shop, and transferred the magic from the artifacts into replicas that I conjured. Since old magic decayed and went *boom*, we saved the artifact and the archaeological site in one go. And we made a tidy profit once we sold the replica.

Once the transfer was done, Cass returned the real artifact to its original resting place. That way, we stayed on the right side of the law and our consciences stayed clean.

Normally, I wouldn't accompany her on a return mission. But I hadn't been able to figure out the strange spell housed in the beaker and hoped that I'd understand it better if I saw the site. Though I'd gotten the magic out of the beaker, it was hard to sell it if we didn't know what it did.

Except that getting to the site was going to be scary as hell.

For one, the sinkhole was massive and deep. On the other side, a thin waterfall fell into the hole, a delicate stream of sparkling liquid disappearing into the darkness below.

Somehow, that only made it creepier. Like we were jumping into the mouth of hell while it was having a drink.

"It's about a hundred feet deep." Cass dug a small headlamp out of her pocket and put it on.

I sucked in a bracing breath. "Then let's get this show on the road."

I called upon my magic, the conjuring gift that I'd worked so hard to perfect. It wasn't my only magic—but it was the only magic I could use that wouldn't get me killed. My FireSoul side was strictly verboten.

My conjuring power swelled within my chest, a warmth that comforted as it created. Magic sparked along my fingertips, and I envisioned climbing gear. Ropes, harnesses, carabiners. I'd had to study up before we'd come out here so I'd conjure the right things.

Fortunately, all answers could be found on the internet. As the pile of equipment appeared at my feet, queasiness roiled in my stomach. I sucked in a breath, trying to quell the illness.

"You okay?" Cass asked.

"Yeah." I breathed through the nausea, wishing it would go away, and bent down to pick up the harness. I handed Cass the red nylon. While she put it on, I secured her line to a sturdy tree.

"Am I good?" she asked.

3

"Yep."

She saluted and dropped down into the hole. If she'd been near her boyfriend, Aidan, she could have mirrored his ability to shift into any animal and flown us down. But he was busy at work, so we were doing this the old-fashioned way. Since we'd made a career of doing it that way, it was no problem.

I followed her lead, putting on my own headlamp and securing my equipment, then lowering myself down against the wall. The wind cut off abruptly as I entered the silent shaft. The stone was slick beneath my feet as we bounced our way down.

"Getting dark down here," Cass called.

"That's how—"

My line snapped. Terror cut off my words as I plummeted through the air. I was still sixty feet above the ground!

I scrabbled for the stone wall, my fingertips grazing the rock.

From below, Cass shrieked. The fear in her voice was nothing compared to the terror racing through me. My skin was ice and my heartbeat thundered.

Help!

I didn't know who I was asking. I clawed for the wall, my fingertips grazing a scraggly green vine. Somehow, I caught hold of it. I gripped it hard, but my weight was too much.

The vine tore in half. I plummeted, my heart in my throat.

I passed Cass, who reached out for me, face stark with fear. Her hand missed me by inches.

The ground was getting so close! My body went numb. In that horrible way of car accidents and tragedy, time slowed as I plunged to my death.

Desperately, I tried to conjure something to help. *Anything.* Before I could even try for a giant cushion below me, something grabbed my flailing wrist, jerking me to a stop. My vision spun as I grabbed onto it, holding on to it like a kid to a candy bar. It felt a bit like rope. Another one grabbed my leg. I dangled in the air, twenty feet above the ground.

"Nix!" Cass cried from above. "Are you all right?

"Yeah." My voice was strangled. I panted as I looked up at my caught wrist.

What the hell was going on?

A vine, or a tree root maybe, had wrapped around my wrist. It was hard to tell in the dark, with just my headlamp flashing as I twisted in the air. Another vine had wrapped around my thigh, holding me aloft like a broken puppet.

Slowly, the vine lowered me to the ground. The blood rushing to my ears was a freight train as I struggled to catch my breath. When my feet touched the ground, I collapsed back against the stone wall of the sinkhole.

"Holy fates." I pressed a hand to my heaving chest, glancing up at Cass.

The vines, or whatever they had been, now lay still against the wall. Cass was lowering herself down, making quick progress. She landed with a thud, then charged me, wrapping her arms around my neck.

"Holy shit, you scared me!" Her words tumbled out. "What the hell was that?"

I pushed her back, still struggling to catch my breath. "No idea. Vines, I think."

Cass looked up. "That's freaking weird. I didn't feel any magic here."

I pulled off my backpack and checked the bubble wrapped based within. Unbroken, thankfully. "It was definitely magic. Unless they were zombie vines."

She arched a brow. "Helpful zombie vines?"

"You're right. Unlikely." But what they were, I had no freaking clue.

"How'd you fall?" Cass asked.

I pulled at the rope attached to my harness, finding it to be completely intact. "That's weird. Maybe I tied it off wrong? Knots have never been my strong suit, and I've never done any rock

5

climbing before."

"Possibly," Cass said.

"Probably." As much as I loved research, it couldn't replace practice. Especially when dangling one hundred feet above the bottom of a stone pit.

Shit. Good thing I hadn't gotten Cass's knots wrong.

"Could someone have untied it?" Cass asked.

I looked up. The opening to the sinkhole seemed to be miles away. "I don't see anyone."

"Let's get a move on, then. I don't like this place. As soon as we return the artifact, I can transport us out of here."

"Good plan, Batman." I turned from the wall and faced the pit.

We were inside a cavern that ballooned out. The light was dim but revealed walls coated in a slick sheen of water. The waterfall fell into a small pool that drained on the far end in a river. There were at least four tunnels that I could see. The river flowed through one.

"Not the river one, right?" I asked.

"Nope, thank fates. Though there will be water later. Come on. We need to get to the other side."

I followed Cass around the edge of the pool. We passed behind the waterfall. I pressed myself against the wall, trying to avoid the spray that splashed coldly against my face. Nausea roiled in my stomach.

Ugh.

I ignored it—it was the only thing I could do. We hurried across the cavern toward one of the smaller tunnels.

"Ah, crap," I muttered. It got a whole lot narrower inside, the roof lowering until we'd clearly have to crawl. We'd barely fit.

"Yeah, it's a tight squeeze," Cass said.

"You're telling me."

"You'll want to take the pack off." Cass tugged her own off.

Sweat dampened my palms. "That tight?"

"A little farther down, yeah."

I pulled my pack off and followed Cass into the tunnel. It was damp and chilly. When I got to my knees and started to crawl, water quickly soaked through my jeans.

Within twenty yards, we were on our bellies. The ceiling was only a few inches over my back. Six at most. I pushed my pack ahead of me on the ground, careful to protect the clay beaker inside.

"I kinda hate this." My heart thundered in my ears as the rock closed in around me.

"Same." Cass shimmied through a particularly tight bit.

I followed, my stomach turning.

By the time the tunnel was big enough to kneel, my skin was crawling. I scrambled after Cass, standing as soon as there was room.

I stumbled almost immediately, my queasy stomach turning my legs to jelly.

"Are you sure you're okay?" Cass said.

"Great." *Lurch.* "Okay, not great." I leaned against the stone wall.

"It's your new magic, isn't it?" Cass asked.

I sucked in a ragged breath. "Yeah. That Destroyer magic feels like it's destroying my insides."

"You've got to learn to control it."

"I know. I just...need time." I'd used my FireSoul power to steal this magic from an evil mage only two days ago. I hadn't wanted to take it—I'd only wanted to take his Informa gift and know what secrets he'd stolen. But I'd gotten both. And now the Destroyer magic was making me sick as a frat boy on a Sunday morning. I'd tried practicing to control it, but hadn't had any luck. "Let's get a move on."

"Fine. But soon as we get home, you're practicing your new magic."

"Yeah, yeah, Mom." I followed her down the corridor, my ears

7

perking up at the sound of voices. It was faint, but... "Do you hear that?"

Cass turned her head, cocking it. "Maybe? It's so faint."

The sound had disappeared. "Let's keep going. But keep your guard up."

"Always."

We hurried through the winding corridor, which opened onto a chamber the size of a small theatre. The ceiling soared fifty feet above. Another tunnel exited the chamber on the far wall. Magic prickled on the air.

"Feel that?" I muttered.

"Yeah, but I don't think—"

The ground rumbled beneath our feet. The sound of stone cracking chilled my skin. Rocks tumbled from the wall as it split and cracked. The sound was deafening. A large boulder thudded in front of the tunnel exit—right where we needed to go.

Shit!

Cass pointed to the ceiling. "Spiders!"

I looked up, dread opening a pit in my stomach.

Massive arachnids crawled out of a hole in the ceiling. They were three feet in diameter if they were an inch—so big that I could see they had *fur*—and their fangs were the size of daggers.

My heart dropped to my feet and my skin chilled. Forcing myself to focus—or get eaten by giant spiders—I conjured my bow and arrow, the weapons so familiar they felt like an extension of my arm.

"Take care of the rocks!" I called. *We had to get out of here.* "I've got the spiders."

One of them descended from the ceiling on its web, multifaceted eyes glinting in the light of my headlamp. This was a horror movie come to life.

I drew an arrow from the ether and fired, piercing the beast between the eyes. I hated killing it, but everyone knew giant spiders only wanted one thing. To wrap you up in their webs and feed off you for days.

And that was a big fat nope for me.

My other *deirfiúr*, Del, always said it was bad luck to kill spiders. But she hadn't been talking about these bad boys.

As Cass raced to the massive boulder, water began to fill the cavern, flowing from the side walls.

"That's not even possible!" Cass shouted. "The river doesn't flow this way."

Magic.

"Were these enchantments here when you came before?" I fired at a spider that scuttled along the wall, taking him out as he neared Cass. He plummeted to the ground, splashing into the water.

"No!" Cass's magic swelled on the air. The scent of ozone crackled. She hurled a lightning bolt at the boulder. Thunder boomed in the cavern, making my head ring.

"Don't hit the water!" I cried.

Fortunately, the bolt had hit high on the stone. A small fissure appeared.

"I know that!" Cass yelled. She hurled another lightning bolt, bigger than the last.

I left her to it, aiming for the spiders that were climbing down the walls, their eyes greedy and riveted to us. The idea of being bound in their web made me shudder.

Water rose to my knees, then my thighs. My heartbeat roared in my ears. Lightning and thunder cracked as Cass tried to blow apart the boulder blocking our exit.

Please don't hit the water.

Between the lightning, water, and spiders, this was getting dire.

Or getting to be a good time. It all depended on the outcome, really.

I fired as fast as I could. My arrows flew through the air,

whistling bullets of death. But there were too many spiders!

One of them caught sight of another that I'd pierced with an arrow. It diverted its path—which had been headed straight for me—and leapt upon the fallen arachnid. It scuttled around the body, splashing in the water as it bound the spider in its web.

Yep—not for me.

I fired at other spiders, barely holding them off as they climbed out of the hole in the ceiling. We were being over-whelmed as Cass's lightning cracked in the air. Our only salvation was the fact that some of the spiders were going for their dead buddies.

Except they probably weren't buddies if they were eating each other.

"Hurry, Cass!" The water was to my waist.

"Almost...there." Cass hurled a bolt of lightning that blinded me with brightness.

Panic over oncoming spiders that I couldn't see chilled my skin. Then the water started to rush away from around me.

"Watch out!" There was a great splash.

Through hazy vision, I saw that Cass had blown through the rock, clearing the tunnel that was our exit. Cass splashed as she was carried out by the rush of water. The body of a spider bobbed by her. Had it knocked her over?

They were rushed out of the room on the torrent of water surging out toward the now-open tunnel.

Something heavy hit me in the side. My feet flew out from under me, and I crashed into the water. My bow was torn from my hands as the current carried me toward the tunnel. I splashed and sputtered, gasping. Beside me, a hairy spider floated.

Ugh. My stomach turned.

"Nix!" Cass's voice echoed. "You...okay?"

The water surged around me, and I sucked in air. "Yeah!"

My headlamp flashed off of the tunnel walls as the river hurtled us through the passage. Finally it began to slow, the level lowering as it dissipated. I slid to a stop on the tunnel floor, the spider's hairy body pressed right up against me. His creepy eyes stared eerily at nothing.

I struggled to my feet, stepping away from him.

Heaviness weighted my chest at the sight of his dead body. "Sorry I had to shoot you."

Cass staggered up, her jeans and brown leather jacket soaking and her red hair straggling around her face. "It's okay. He was going to eat you. Slowly. Don't feel bad."

"Yeah, yeah. I know." And I really didn't want to be eaten—slowly or not. I turned from the body, spying my conjured bow about five feet down the way. I picked it up, inspecting it for damage. Still good.

I looked up at Cass. "Let's get a move on."

"Couldn't agree more."

I shivered against the chill air that made my wet clothes feel icy. As I walked down the passage, I pulled my pack off my back and inspected the wrapped beaker within.

"How is it?" Cass asked.

"Still good." I couldn't see it well through the bubble wrap, but it didn't look broken.

Cass hurried to catch up. "Soon as we return the artifact, we can transport right out of here."

"It's a shame we can't just transport there."

"No can do. Magical protections." Cass laughed lightly. "Which was smart of the original inhabitants, considering how many artifacts are back there."

Something unfamiliar sounded from behind me. "Do you hear that?"

"Kinda. Voices?"

"Eh, that's not good."

If there were voices, then maybe I hadn't screwed up my knot. Maybe they'd untied it. Which meant this wasn't a caving club out for an adventure.

I picked up the pace, trotting along the corridor. Fortunately, it was wider than that terrifying belly-crawl one from earlier.

"We're nearly there." Cass pointed to the end of the tunnel, which was smaller and narrower.

We ducked through. Light from my headlamp cut through the cavern, shining off of dozens of golden and copper artifacts that were placed on large tables made of stone. Jewelry and cups, daggers and buttons. Gold, copper, bronze. The table had probably been hewn from the rock walls thousands of years ago.

There were hundreds of beakers as well, small clay vases that gave this culture their name. No doubt they hadn't called themselves the Beaker people, but in the last three thousand years, their true names had been lost.

I didn't know if the human Beaker people had built their tombs—or whatever this was—in caves, but the supernaturals had.

Many of the artifacts gave off magical signatures of all varieties. Scents of grass and dirt along with the feel of wind and rain. But none of the magic felt decayed, like our beaker's had. Which meant all of these would stay put.

I dug the bubble-wrapped package out of my bag and unwrapped it, revealing a small vase made of rough clay. Simple designs were imprinted on the surface.

Cass pointed to a blank space on the table in the middle of the room. "It was sitting right there."

I approached, focusing my senses on the magical signatures that bombarded me from all sides. Whatever magic this beaker had contained, it was unidentifiable. Hoping for clues, I inspected the empty space where it had sat, along with the golden bracelets on either side and the three other beakers at the back.

"I'm getting nothing." I sighed as I set the beaker down. It'd been a long shot anyway.

I turned to face Cass.

Shit!

From the tunnel entrance behind her, figures poured into the room.

"Cass!" I cried.

She whirled to face the oncoming threat. There were a dozen of them. All demons. Each was at least seven feet tall. They were all skinny and pale, with massively long claws and eyes of pure white. They didn't carry any weapons, but they wouldn't need them with their Wolverine-looking claws.

I drew my bow, conjuring an arrow. As Cass sent a blast of lightning at the demon nearest her, I fired, piercing mine through his eye.

But the demons were fast, charging us. Too close for my bow. As I conjured a sword to fight the nearest demon, two human figures stepped out of the tunnel.

Both men. One had scraggly black hair and sallow skin. There was a tattoo on his neck, but I could only see a tiny bit because of his collar and couldn't say what it was.

He raised a hand. Magic swelled in the air, feeling like bugs crawling across my skin. A crack opened in the ceiling, and giant spiders flowed out.

Shit! The creepy mage was responsible for the spiders. I didn't even have time to focus on them. The demon nearest me lunged. I sliced out with my sword, taking off his hand. He howled. I stabbed him in the gut, then yanked my blade free.

Across the way, Cass was hurling lightning at any demon who approached. She tried to hit the mage, but a demon threw himself in front of the guy, taking the bolt of lightning for his master.

The other mage, who had limp blond hair and watery blue eyes, raised his hands, muttering something under his breath. His magic flowed, tasting like dust in my mouth.

What the hell was he trying to do? Fear chilled my skin.

"Get the beaker!" the dust mage shouted.

Not our beaker? Shit.

I tried to keep my gaze on the spiders climbing down the

walls. Demons came at me from both sides. I managed to stab one, but another got me in the thigh with his claws. Pain flared as he sliced through muscle.

I brought my blade around just as he was reaching for my waist. The shining steel severed his arm.

Stone began to crack and crumble around us. A boulder dropped to the ground, crashing between me and Cass.

"Time to get out of here!" Cass shouted.

"Yeah!" We were *so* outnumbered. There were still five demons, numerous spiders, two insane mages, and now falling boulders.

I stabbed a slender demon in the chest, yanking my blade free, and ran for Cass.

She raced to me, colliding into my chest and then wrapping her arms around me. Her magic swelled on the air, and the ether sucked us in, throwing us through space.

It spat us out on the street in front of our apartment. It was chilly in the late afternoon, with dark clouds obscuring the sun. Skeletal trees lined the park to the left, reaching toward the sky with bony branches. I stumbled away from Cass, wincing at the pain in my leg. The cold winter wind cut through my wet clothes, sending shivers across my skin.

But at least we were out of there.

"Who the hell were they?" Cass's eyes were wide.

"No idea." I inspected the wound, which bled sluggishly. "I think they were after the same beaker we returned."

"Yeah." These demons—or their master—was determined. "But we took the magic out."

"Maybe they didn't know that."

"Or they want the beaker itself. But that doesn't make a lot of sense."

Shit. Del. She was watching the shop. Alone. She'd agreed to do it while I went to the tomb with Cass to try to figure out the beaker's magic.

I met Cass's gaze. Understanding lit her eyes.

"Del." Her voice was stark. Worried.

"Let's go." I started off down the street, Cass racing at my side. Though my wound screamed, fear for Del pushed me on.

As we neared Ancient Magic, the uneasy feeling grew. Not the usual nausea from the Destroyer magic, but something else.

The sight of the broken glass glittering on the street just made it worse.

"Shit." I raced forward.

One of the big windows was broken—the one with Ancient Magic painted in gold. Within, the place was ransacked. Artifact replicas were scattered all over the floor, some broken and their magic gone.

Del, who stood in the middle, turned to face us, her black hair flying. Her blue eyes widened at the sight of us. "Guys."

"How many were there?" Cass asked.

Had to be over a dozen if they were going to overpower Del. My gaze raked her, relieved to find only a few small wounds that seeped blood.

"Fifteen. Maybe more." Del's face crumbled with disappointment. A cut on her cheek dripped blood. "They got the replica of the beaker you just returned."

"Yeah. I figured. But at least you're okay." I stepped inside the shop, careful to avoid the shards of a shattered Ming vase replica. Thankfully, the original artifacts hadn't been destroyed, but we'd lost a lot of magic—and money—in the replicas that had been broken.

"That means they have both," Cass said. "The real one and the replica." Quickly, she explained to Del what had happened at the cave on the Yorkshire Dales.

"Dang." Del scowled.

"So whatever they want to do with that magic, they can do." I scrubbed a weary hand over my eyes. "We may not know what it does, but I sure as hell don't want them having it."

"Same." Del crouched down and picked up a replica stone arrowhead. It was a Clovis point, the oldest type in the US, and at least it hadn't broken. Its ability to predict the weather remained intact. She squeezed it, her gaze darkening. "We need to find those bastards."

I wracked my brain, trying to remember what the mages had looked like when they'd ambushed us in the cave. They'd been the bosses. The demons were just their hired muscle. "Did you see a dragon tattoo on either of those mages? I saw something, but it could have been a tattoo of anything."

"I missed it," Cass said. "And what are the odds, anyway?"

"Nope, nothing," Del said.

"Yeah, you're right," I said. "There's no reason to think they're connected. I'm just paranoid."

A few days ago, we'd learned of the existence of some kind of mob boss whose minions all wore dragon tattoos. Though we didn't know what the guy's goal was, we wanted to. But it was a stretch to think they were connected.

A car door slammed from behind me and I turned. Roarke, Del's boyfriend, climbed out of his black Tesla. Concern shadowed his face, drawing his dark brows together.

"Are you okay?" He hurried to Del.

"It's just a flesh wound." She hugged him.

I grinned at her Monty Python joke, one I was quite fond of making myself.

Roarke stepped back and surveyed the place. "Bastards."

"Ain't that the truth." I stepped forward to pick up a fallen sword, but the pain in my leg made me wince. I straightened, giving a moment for it to calm down. "We need to find them."

Del's eyes widened as she looked out onto the street. "Uh, Nix. You better turn around. Someone is here for you."

Dread chilled my skin as I turned. I knew what I'd see. And I wasn't going to like it.

CHAPTER TWO

As expected, I didn't like what I saw.

On the sidewalk stood Ares Warhaven, the ridiculously powerful and sexy vampire who was currently a giant thorn in my side. Actually, he was more like a stake in my side. A huge one.

I kinda wanted to pull it out and stab him, but wood didn't hurt vampires unless Hollywood wielded the stake.

As usual, he wore dark jeans, boots, and a black shirt that was supposed to be casual but looked like haute couture on his huge frame. He had a warrior's build—tall and strong with a stance that was ready to pounce—and a warrior's face. Ruggedly handsome, but with a calm deadliness to the set of his features.

His green eyes pierced me, making my stupid heart flutter. This guy held my life in his hands, and I didn't like it. But still, my dumb hormones were off on their own agenda again.

He stepped forward, surveying the damage. "What happened here?"

His deep voice, tinged lightly with an accent that was distinctly vampiric, sent a second shiver down my spine.

I really needed to call a cease-fire on all shivers. My body couldn't be trusted.

"Robbery." I eyed him. "It's time already? It's only been a couple days. You said I'd have a week."

His timing was pure shit, what with this robbery and all.

His gaze met mine, mysterious and deep. "I said I'd try to get you a week. But the Vampire Court will not wait. It's time to prove your loyalty."

My shoulders slumped. Damn.

"What the hell is he talking about?" Cass demanded.

Del stepped between me and Ares, a human shield. "Back off, dude."

He smiled, not the least bit threatened. Anyone with an ounce of sense *should* feel threatened by Del or Cass—they were hard-core badasses who struck first and asked questions later —but Ares...

He was damned tough himself. As the strongest vampire alive and half mage, he wouldn't be easy to take down.

Which was why I'd agreed to his terms. Terms I now had to explain to my *deirfiúr*.

I turned to Cass and Nix. "I'm sorry. I was going to tell you. I thought I had a week."

Understanding dawned in Cass's green eyes. "This is because he knows you're a FireSoul."

I nodded. "And Doyen and Magisteria know, too."

Between the three of them, that was the whole Vampire Court, which meant a *whole* lot of trouble for me.

I drew in a breath. "They've agreed not to turn me in to the Order of the Magica." Which basically saved my skin, since the Order would toss me in the Prison for Magical Miscreants. "At least, as long as I complete their interview and trials."

"Interview and trials?" Del nearly shrieked the words.

"Bullshit." Cass scowled at Ares.

"We need to know that we can trust her. FireSouls have a...
certain reputation."

"For murdering and stealing powers. Yeah, that's not news,"
I said.

"And you know Nix," Del said. "You know she'd never
do that."

He nodded. "I'm almost sure of that."

Almost? Ouch. So he didn't fully trust me.

Which he'd said before, but I hadn't liked hearing it. But then,
it wasn't like I trusted *him*.

"But Doyen and Magisteria don't know her," Ares said. "They
need proof they're not letting a murderer go free. A magic
stealer. Not to mention, she can walk in the Shadowlands. Something that should be impossible for her."

"It's fine, guys." I held up a hand to stop their words. "If I
complete the trials—which I will—I'll have Vampire Court
protection."

We could really use them on our side. Maybe they'd back us if
the Order ever found out what we were.

"Is this true?" Cass demanded. "You'd protect her then?"

He nodded, his gaze solemn. It was so serious that in that
moment, I *did* trust him. At least in this.

Roarke stepped forward. He was as big as Ares, but his
features more refined. "But she has to pass your trials." His gaze
met mine, concern in their dark depths. "Do you know what's
coming for you? Because it won't be easy."

"I can take it."

"I hope so." Roarke frowned at Ares. "Did you tell her that
only half of all who attempt it survive?"

Guilt flashed in Ares's eyes.

"Jerk!" I glared at him. "Why the hell didn't you tell me that?"

"Because you don't have a choice. You must complete these
trials, or the Court *will* turn you in to the Order." He stepped

forward, stopping a few feet from me. "And you will succeed. I've seen you in action. You can handle this."

Still, it was risky. But he was right. I didn't have a choice. I didn't want to run, and I didn't want to go to prison.

That left one option—passing the damned trials and convincing the Vampire Court that I wasn't a monster.

"And I'll be at your side," Ares said. "I'll help you however I can."

"I don't want your help," I snapped. He'd withheld valuable information from me. Could I trust him after that? It didn't matter if I was attracted to him—that was nothing more than hormones and stupidity.

"Doesn't matter. You have it anyway." He gestured toward the open door. "Are you ready to meet the Vampire Court?"

I looked around the shop. At my *deirfiúr*. Then turned to Ares. "Give us a moment, okay?"

He nodded, stepping back out onto the street. Once he was out of earshot, I turned to Del and Cass.

"What are we going to do about this robbery?" I whispered. "I want to help hunt them."

"We can do it," Cass said. "You go deal with these trials. Del and I will get started trying to find the thieves."

"We're the best ones for the job, anyway," Del said. "I actually saw the robbers here, and Cass saw them back at the cavern. That'll help us track them."

She was right. They were both as qualified as me. More so, even.

And I *had* to pass the vampire's tests. Because if I didn't, I'd take my *deirfiúr* down with me. Ares didn't know they were Fire-Souls, too, but it was a punishable crime to harbor one. And once they were in custody for that, the Order would figure out what they were.

Worse, their powerful boyfriends, Roarke and Aidan, would

no doubt wage war to save them. Which would end up creating even more problems.

So, yeah. I was up shit creek, and Ares was poking holes in my boat.

"Okay." I sighed. "You guys hunt the jerks who stole from us. I'll deal with the Vampire Court."

"Show them what you're made of," Cass said.

"Knock their socks off." Del punched me lightly on the arm.

"And know that we're here if you need us." Cass reached out and hugged me.

Del joined in. "Yeah, just give us a call on the comms charm and we'll come kick some vampire ass."

I pulled away. "You know I don't want you to do that."

"Yeah, yeah." Cass waved her hand. "Starting an interspecies war would be a bad idea."

"Exactly." I grinned, then turned, waving as I walked out. "Time to meet my destiny."

Ares's gaze snapped up to meet mine. "Is that me?"

"You weren't supposed to hear that." I zipped my jacket up, but it was still so wet it did little good. Fear over Del had made me forget that I was soaking wet. The cold reminded me. "I need to stop by my place and get cleaned up."

As we walked, the pain in my leg grew.

"You're hurt." Concern shadowed Ares's voice.

"It's nothing." I reached my door and shoved the key in. The lock snicked, and I pushed it open, stepping inside.

Ares followed, but I spun and held out a hand. "You wait here."

A brow arched. "You let me in before."

"That was before you dropped the interview and trials bombshell on me. Now, I'm wary."

He nodded. "Then at least let me look at your leg."

"No."

But he'd already dropped to his knees. I gasped, stepping back. He reached out, catching the back of my uninjured thigh with his big hand and holding me steady. The heat of his palm burned through my cold jeans, racing up my body and filling my lower belly with warmth. Goosebumps prickled on my impossibly sensitive skin.

Despite the throbbing pain in the wound on my right thigh, my breath caught in my throat. At this distance, I could smell his fresh winter scent and feel the magic that rolled off him like a caress.

All kinds of dirty things flashed in my mind—like what he could do down there.

No. Stupid.

"I'm fine." I tugged, but he held me firm.

He tilted his head, inspecting the wound. "It's deep."

His raspy voice made me shiver, then shock followed. "Are you turned on by my blood?"

He cleared his throat, then glanced up at me, darkness in his gaze. Disappointment, too. But that was weird.

"It's complicated." He drew in a ragged breath. "It's my nature to be attracted to your blood. But when it comes from a wound…" Disgust laced his voice. "I can't help the desire, but I hate that it comes from something that caused you pain."

Oh. Huh.

I curled my fingers into a fist, resisting the desire to sink my hand into his dark hair.

This was all kinds of fucked up.

"Let me heal it," he said.

I sucked in a shuddery breath, remembering the last time he'd healed me with his blood. It'd been…*intimate.* In a position like this? After he'd just confessed to being turned on by my blood?

I could almost feel the conflicting emotions coming off of him. Desire, disgust. He hated this about himself, but couldn't help it. And pain. Pain for my wound—for the hurt that I suffered from it. There was darkness all around him.

Whoa.

I stepped back, pulling myself from his grip. This was too much. Too close.

"I'll be back," I said. "You stay here."

He surged to his feet, but something in my expression must have stayed him. He curled his big hands into fists, nodding sharply.

I turned and ran up the stairs, limping with every step.

"Don't hurt yourself." The command in his voice made me shiver.

I slipped into my apartment and leaned back against the door.

Holy crap, what had that been?

I'd never been so attracted to another person. But that had also been *weird*. And the way I'd felt his emotions?

Damn.

I thought I'd felt something similar last week—his sadness over losing his friend Marin. But this had been even more intense.

I wasn't an empath though. That was a specific type of magical being, and it certainly wasn't me. If anything, I was pretty damned dense about other people.

Was it because he'd healed me with his blood before?

It made sense, but who even knew? Certainly not me.

I shook my head, trying to banish the memory of him kneeling in front of me, his warm hand on my thigh, burning me from the inside.

I stumbled toward my bathroom. It was tiny and old, having just enough room for a small vanity, shower, and toilet. I knelt in front of the vanity, my thigh screaming in pain, and dug through my supplies for a healing tonic. A while ago, I'd made some using the magical plants in my trove. If I was lucky, I'd have some left.

Jackpot.

My fingers closed around a slender glass vase. I pulled it free,

23

uncorking it with shaking hands, then twisted around to pour the liquid over the wound.

It sizzled and singed, making tears sting my eyes, but it did the job. Slowly, the flesh knit back together. I didn't like to use this unless I had to—it took years to make—but I'd categorize this as being absolutely necessary.

I certainly wasn't going to let him heal me again, and Cass's boyfriend, Aidan, was in Europe on work, so he couldn't heal me.

Once the potion stopped bubbling, I recorked the vial and pulled off my clothes. A quick look in the mirror showed that my skin was pale but my cheeks bright red. My eyes were giant saucers, the pupils blown out to encapsulate my eyes.

I sucked in a ragged breath, leaning over the vanity and trying to get my shit together.

I could do this.

Two goals: pass the Vampire Court's trials and avoid Ares Warhaven.

Because whatever we had between us—it was too intense for me.

I shoved away from the counter and cranked on the shower, setting it to boiling. My wet clothes were a nightmare to remove, but finally I was able to hop into the water.

Closing my eyes, I let it wash away the blood and the dirt and hopefully the memory of Ares on his knees.

The first two disappeared; the third didn't. I hopped out and dried off quickly, then ransacked my closet for clean T-shirt and jeans. When I found my Maru shirt, I grinned. I loved that Japanese box cat.

I tugged on my clothes, finishing with the shirt and a leather jacket from the back of my closet. For good measure, I shoved the bottle of healing potion in my pocket.

A glance at my clock showed that getting cleaned up had only taken ten minutes.

That left me enough time to visit my trove. The thought of it made me tremble. Just a few minutes. That was all I wanted. I was like an addict jonesing for a fix—my desire to hang out with my preciouses overwhelming my FireSoul side.

I hurried to the other side of the room, my leg no longer paining me, and pressed my hands to the wall. I fed it my magic, igniting the spell that made the wall disappear. A doorway formed, and I stepped through, then climbed the spiral staircase to the roof.

When I stepped out into the jungle of my trove, a sigh escaped me. Tension seeped from my muscles as I ran my fingertips over the leaves of an elephant fern. Greens in every shade exploded around me, dotted with brilliant color from the blooms of every flower I'd ever seen.

In the middle of the space sat my three babies—the cars that I loved so much. But it was the plants that drew me today. I couldn't get enough of touching the petals and leaves, the bark and roots.

Normally, I wasn't so drawn to the plants. I loved them, but I didn't feel like I had to roll around in them. Now, they comforted me. Calming my racing heart and pushing away the memories of Ares. Even my limbs felt stronger.

After a few minutes, I felt well enough to go.

"Thanks, guys," I murmured, petting the petal of an orange orchid.

As I climbed down from the roof, my mind raced. What was coming for me? Ares said he'd be on my side, but did he mean it?

By the time I made it out of my apartment and down the stairs, Ares was leaning against the doorjamb.

His gaze darted immediately to my thigh. "You're not limping."

"I took care of it."

"How? You have no healing."

"I had a potion." I wouldn't share which one. He didn't need to know about my trove either. Even though he knew I was a Fire-

Soul—and perhaps knew what that entailed—I wasn't letting him in on my secrets just yet. "Will you transport us?"

He nodded, then held out a hand.

My breath stuck in my throat as I reached for it. When his warm grip encapsulated mine, I realized just how big he really was. Particularly when he tugged me toward him. He towered over me like this.

Since he wasn't the type of guy to throw his weight around—puffing out his chest and all that crap—it was sometimes easy to forget that he was a massive freaking warrior and the strongest vampire alive.

In my experience, it was always the deadliest guys who didn't need to brag about their strength. Ares fit that bill perfectly.

"Ready?" His voice was soft above my head, as if he, too, were affected by our closeness.

But I was no longer bleeding, so that was weird.

"Yeah," I croaked.

A moment later, the ether sucked us in. Dizziness assaulted me. Too much transporting in too short a time.

When I opened my eyes, we were in the dark. It took a moment for my gaze to adjust. A heavy moon sat high in the sky, shedding light over the trees around us. They were massive. Like great redwoods, but their bark was black. The leaves that were far overhead glittered silver in the moonlight.

"Wow." I spun in a circle, taking in my surroundings. We stood on a circular white marble floor that was about sixty feet across. Trees surrounded us on all sides but left room for the light of the moon to shine off the marble. Light gray stone was inlaid to form a nine-pointed star. It gleamed, but not as brightly as the massive gate ahead of me.

The thing was thirty feet tall if it was an inch, a giant archway leading to a path that wound through the forest. It was built of shining white marble. Roses climbed up the sides, their leaves a deep green and their blooms dark red.

They looked like blood.

Weirdly, the whole scene was rather beautiful. Though my eyes adjusted to the light, shadows pressed in on me from all sides. "It's dark here."

"We're called the Court of Night for a reason." Ares gestured to the gate. "Are you ready?"

"This is the entrance to your realm?"

"Sort of. It starts here, on this platform. We cannot transport inside because it is a security risk. So we'll walk." He headed toward the archway, then stepped beneath and passed onto the path beyond.

I followed, my skin prickling as I crossed under. Magic and power snapped against my skin, almost like a protection charm was trying to repel me. But it was more than that. Magic. Might. Good and bad. Light and dark.

I had no idea what to make of it.

Ares stood on the path, watching me. Interest glinted in his dark eyes.

"This is another test, isn't it? Like when you watched me enter the Shadowlands." It was the part of Magic's Bend that was owned by the vampires. The same interest had gleamed in his eyes—curiosity to know how I could pass into that area when I was neither vampire nor had I been given permission by the Vampire Court as one of their allies.

"It is." A reluctant smile tugged at his mouth. It was so tiny that I thought I imagined it. But the grim expression that slashed over his features wasn't hard to miss. "You're powerful, Phoenix Knight. Too powerful for an unknown."

A chill raced down my spine. "I'm not."

"Anomalies are usually powerful."

"Weirdos, you mean." I pointed a finger at him. "Like you. Half vampire, half mage."

"Like me." He turned and started down the path.

I followed, hurrying to keep up with his long stride. Being six and a half feet tall gave the guy an advantage there.

The massive trees were as wide as houses and lined the path that we walked. They were even bigger than redwoods, I realized. Dinosaurs of their smaller earth cousins.

In front of them stood white marble statues. Animals of all varieties.

Beasts, really.

Mythical beasts—and only the strongest, most deadly ones. There were hydras and minotaurs and giant scorpions and two-headed wolves—but no mystical hamsters or bunny rabbits.

Even more noticeable was the magic that drifted off of the statues, like an air freshener meant to say *Beware—We're Fucking Scary.*

And they were. It was the kind of magic that put the thought of lost souls and battle and blood into my mind. Like these guys would jump to life if I put one toe out of line.

After the sheer beauty of the entryway, the statues were freaking scary.

It was a dichotomy that was so similar to Ares. Beautiful, but terrifying.

"You guys are really obsessed with power, aren't you?" I asked.

He nodded sharply. "Strength is important to vampires. We're predators. *The* apex predator."

"And you're the strongest one of them all."

He didn't respond, but I knew I was right. In the moonlight, his hair gleamed with a dark sheen. His skin, usually pale, glowed with light. For the first time since entering his realm, I inspected him more closely. He looked even better in this light. Stronger, more dangerous.

The fact that I liked the dangerous side more was bad news. I was one sick cookie.

But I couldn't look away. His cheekbones were sharper and

his eyes harder. The muscles that moved fluidly beneath his shirt were more pronounced. Cut from iron.

I swallowed hard.

This place changed Ares. Making him harder, stronger, colder. Maybe it was just my imagination, but if so, my imagination was damned good. Because he definitely seemed scarier here.

And I wasn't used to being afraid.

Afraid for my *deirfiúr*, sure. But for myself? Not normally. Not until this guy had come into my life.

And yet my body still hummed for him.

Which I was going to ignore. One look at his hard eyes, the ruthless set of his shoulders, and it was easy.

CHAPTER THREE

Unease prickled along my skin as we walked down the moonlit path. The power emitted by the statues was being replaced with something else.

"We're close, aren't we?"

"Yes."

The path ended at another white stone archway. It was twenty feet tall and covered in a climbing vine of lilies.

I glanced at Ares. "You going to watch me walk through this one, too?"

He shook his head. "There's no special magic here. You're fully inside our realm."

"Good." I stepped through, expecting to see a large stone building or other administrative center. But there was only a garden.

A fabulous, night-blooming garden with all sorts of plants that I'd never seen before. Moonlight glowed brightly on the blooms, as if the petals sucked up the light and reflected it back.

"This place is amazing." I touched the petal of an ornate yellow flower.

An electric current zipped up my finger. I yanked it back and laughed.

"That didn't hurt?" Ares asked.

"No. Felt funny."

"Hmm." A thoughtful look entered his eyes.

"Was it supposed to hurt?"

"Normally. Most plants here are dangerous. Poison or otherwise."

"Not that little guy." I gave it one more stroke, then turned to Ares. He stood in front of an enormous silver fern. The color was almost like his eyes when he was in full vampire mode. "Where's the building?"

"No building. Not here. When the night moon is full, we prefer to be out under it."

I'd been expecting some kind of ornate castle. "Well, I guess if that's the only light you're ever going to get..." Except for Ares and his unique ability to walk under the sun—I bet all the vampires wished they were half-breeds. I gestured for him to continue. "Let's get this over with."

"Excited?"

"Hardly."

A small smile tugged at the corner of his mouth and he turned, leading me down one of the narrower paths. The magic that floated on the air was uncomfortable, like prickles against my skin.

When we reached a clearing, it was obvious where the magic was coming from.

To the left, three massive white thrones sat amongst a profusion of white rose bushes. They were ornately carved, with swirling designs of ivory. True masterpieces of delicate carving. They faced a large lake that was covered in silver-tipped waves. It was more of a sea, really.

Within the thrones sat Doyen and Magisteria. The third was empty—presumably for Ares. The beautiful vampires were reading, though I'd bet money they weren't the mystery novels I preferred.

Though they were sitting casually, sipping a blood-red liquid, their magic rolled off them like waves.

The message was clear: *Beware, ye who approach.*

No problem.

Their coldness, their clear willingness to cut down any who defied them, was apparent from their magic. I hadn't felt it as strongly before, but here, in their own world, it was as cold as a steel blade against my throat.

"What magic do they have?" I whispered.

"Doyen, mind reading and some mind control. Manipulating emotions. Magisteria can control the bodies of others. Like puppets. It works best in this realm, as she is made stronger by the magic here."

I gasped, then shuddered. *No.* What a terrible power.

Ares stepped forward. "Magisteria. Doyen."

They glanced up, their gazes cold. Their features were sharper, icier, than they had been when I'd seen them on earth. The same change Ares had gone through. I saw something else of Ares in them as well—that icy ability to do a job and do it right. To be a ruler.

But he wasn't like them. He was different.

Right?

I glanced at him. He fit in well here.

"She came willingly?" Doyen's red hair reflected in the moonlight. She was still eerily beautiful, but with her creepy magic rolling off of her, it was unsettling.

"Of course," I said. "Those were the terms."

Doyen shrugged. "Most don't want to attempt our trials."

"They're smart," Magisteria said. "You…"

The implication was obvious.

"I'm brave." I stepped forward. "And I'm not worried about whatever you're going to throw at me."

Teeny tiny lie.

"You should be," Ares said.

"We'll just see about that." I approached the thrones, my gaze traveling between Doyen and Magisteria. Up close, I realized that their intricately carved white thrones were made of *bone*.

Freaking yikes.

I swallowed hard. "So, what do you want from me?"

Ares passed me, taking his seat on the far left side. Though he'd said he didn't like to spend much time in this realm, he looked at home in his creepy throne.

Though I didn't trust him, I really wished he was at my side right now.

"We want to know why you can walk in the Shadowlands," Magisteria said. "That should be forbidden to one who isn't among our allies."

I shrugged. "No idea."

"We'll figure it out," Ares said. "But first—a test to prove you are loyal."

"To you?"

"Of course," Magisteria said.

Hmmm. I wasn't sure about that. What did loyalty entail? I wouldn't hurt them, sure. But I also didn't want to do their bidding. But I kept my mouth shut. Better to play it close to the vest.

"How do I prove that?" I asked.

"A task." Doyen stood. "There is a treasure in a volcano at the far end of our realm. Use your skills to bring the treasure to us."

"What kind of treasure?"

"You will see," Magisteria said.

"I will accompany you," Ares said. "To monitor your progress. I will help you until you reach the volcano, but then you are on your own."

"Okay. I can handle that. But do you guys have any clues

33

about what kind of treasure I'm looking for? This is pretty broad."

Magisteria reached for the golden goblet she had been sipping from. She crooked her finger at me.

She was very impressed with herself, this one.

I approached, feeling her magical signature grow as I neared. It prickled and stung.

She handed me the goblet. "That is your clue."

"Gold?"

"Of a sort."

"What the hell does that mean?"

"You'll figure it out. But that is your only clue."

"Fine." I focused my dragon sense on the goblet, assuming they wanted more of the yellow metal. It shined brightly in the light of the moon, smooth and lovely. Though I didn't consider gold to be treasure—that was reserved for plants, cars, and weapons—my dragon sense *loved* gold.

Stereotype City, population: me.

But it meant that it was much easier to find gold than anything else.

Where did you come from?

It took a moment, but my magic latched on. The familiar tug pulled from around my middle, dragging me to the right. To an area far away. Dozens of miles. Maybe a hundred.

"There's more of this far away," I said. "In that volcano, right?"

"Yes." Ares stood. "I'll transport us partway there. Now that we are within the realm, I can transport again. Once there, we begin."

We. Until we reached the volcano and he ditched me. "Great. Let's get this party started."

I handed the goblet back to Magisteria, my fingertips itching as I handed it over. My dragon soul really didn't want to part with it.

"I'm surprised by your enthusiasm," Doyen said. "Only a fraction of the people who attempt our trials survive."

"You underestimate me." Still, fear shivered along my spine. I was brave, not stupid. But I wasn't going to let this creepy chick see my fear. I turned to Ares. "Ready?"

"Absolutely." He stood and turned to Doyen and Magisteria. "Until later."

They nodded, then picked up their books. They were reading as we walked away, toward the woods, and, I assumed, a place to transport.

"Well, this will be fun," I said.

He glanced down at me. "Don't underestimate the challenges ahead."

"Do you know what they are?" I followed him down the path we'd come, back through the statues lining the way.

"No. In situations like these, two of the court create the challenge. The third accompanies the initiate to observe progress."

"Doesn't that put you in danger?"

"It does, but that's what this allyship entails. You are proving yourself, but we do the same. A partnership, of sorts. Both sides are at risk."

"Interesting. But if many of the initiates don't survive, yet you guys have been sitting pretty on your thrones for years... That means you step back if I get in a deadly situation."

"It does." He frowned. "At least, we're supposed to. We cannot accept the weak or stupid into our numbers."

We're supposed to? Did that mean he didn't want to step back if I ended up in danger? But he'd ditched me and sat on that throne.

I was clearly imagining things.

"You've sure got a nice throne," I prodded.

He grimaced. "Tradition. Though Doyen and Magisteria like them very much."

He turned to me. "Ready to transport?"

I stepped toward him and took his hand. A moment later, the

35

ether sucked us in. My head spun as we were transported across his realm. When I felt solid land beneath my feet, I opened my eyes.

Shit.

The forest surrounding us was darker and creepier than the one we'd been in before, but the trees were just as huge. This time, though, the leaves were a dull, dark gray instead of silver. Something sick and dark lurked in the air, a black mist that hovered over the ground. The air was hot and cold at once, like currents were flowing on the wind.

It smelled of volcano, sulphur and heat, burning my nose.

"This place is nice," I joked. "You come here often?"

Ares huffed a laugh. "No. It's cursed. There is a *Burtnieki*—a wizard—who lives deep in the forest. He went mad long ago, and his magic turned dark. He holed up in a castle, but his magic has tainted this place."

"Why did he go mad?"

"He fell in love with Laima, one of our goddesses of fate. He attempted to woo her, but she rejected him."

I shrugged. "Fair enough. So she didn't like the guy."

"I agree. He's rather...unlikeable."

"Entitled, right? Then he got all obsessed and stuff?" It was a tale as old as time.

Annoyance glinted in Ares's eyes. "Essentially. She tried to let him down easy, but he wouldn't take no for an answer. Finally, she ended up predicting his fate publicly. That he would die alone and angry."

"And she was right."

Ares nodded. "Now he's holed up in his castle, pissed at the world and polluting this forest with his malevolence."

"Complaining that girls don't like nice guys," I muttered. Moron. Of course we liked nice guys. Who didn't? There just had to be *more*. Like compatibility and intelligence and attraction. That spark.

Like what she felt with Ares.

Whoa, Nelly!

My horse was getting seriously off track. I shoved any attraction I felt for Ares into a deep, dark corner of my mind. "Let's get a move on. This place is giving me the willies."

Ares nodded. "Lead the way."

I called upon my dragon sense, remembering the golden goblet. It tugged around my waist, pulling me through the forest.

The trees loomed all around as we walked across the spongy ground. The layer of gray leaves rustled underfoot, and the sound of buzzing night insects and cawing birds created a soundtrack that was distinctly *Haunted Forest.*

The dark mist that drifted around our ankles was chilly. In the distance, black snakes slithered around the bases of the trees, but they ignored us.

Still, their beady black eyes were nerve-racking.

I kept my gaze on the forest floor ahead. There was a trail of pounded dirt about twenty yards away.

"There," I said. "That'll take us."

And get us away from the awful mist. I hated the way it—

The ground beneath me rumbled, shifting. I fell, but before I could hit my knees, something twisted around my ankles. Hard.

And pulled me to the ground.

Snakelike roots burst out of the earth, wrapping me in a cocoon that encapsulated my entire body. Every inch was covered, even my eyes. The roots began to squeeze, compressing my lungs until I saw stars.

A scream burst from my lips, but it was no more than a whimper. I'd lost all my breath.

I thrashed, trying to break free. I couldn't move an inch—not even my arms. Desperate, I conjured a blade. I strained, trying to slash at the roots. But it did no good. I couldn't move an inch.

Panic flared in my chest as the roots squeezed tighter. Bark cut into my cheeks and neck. My vision blackened.

Let me go! I screamed inside my mind, compelled by something I didn't understand. *Release me!*

At first, nothing happened.

And then slowly, the roots began to loosen. They slithered away like snakes, until I lay on the forest floor, stunned.

My vision returned after my first hard gasp of air. I sucked the sweet stuff into my lungs, scrambling to my feet. I kept my conjured dagger in my hand, just in case.

"Ares!" I whirled, searching.

He was fifteen feet away, fighting off roots like a whirlwind of speed and muscle. His shadow sword, which he must have drawn from the ether, flew left and right, slicing roots to pieces. A scatter of broken ones lay around him—he must have burst free with his ridiculous vampire strength. But the tree wouldn't stop coming. Roots burst from the ground, lashing at him.

"Stop!" I screamed. "Now!"

Ares looked at me like I was nuts, his brows raised almost to his hairline, but the roots stopped attacking. They slipped back under the dirt like the Kraken returning to the depths of the sea.

Ares stepped forward, his gaze incredulous. "What the hell did you do?"

"I don't know!" I searched the area, but all the roots were silent, far under the ground. The forest floor didn't even look disturbed. "What kind of spell was that?"

"I don't know. One of the wizard's enchantments, perhaps."

"That guy sure doesn't want visitors, does he?"

"Apparently not. But how did you command the tree to stop its attack?" Ares approached, his brows drawn.

"I have no idea. Are you sure it was even me?" *It had definitely been me.*

And Ares was no dummy. "Of course it was you. Those roots burst off you like you were made of acid and stopped their attack as soon as you yelled."

"I don't know—" I wobbled, nausea filling my stomach with what felt like rancid oil. *Ugh.*

Ares stepped forward, steadying me. "Are you all right?"

I ignored the concern in his voice, trying to force the nausea away. "Yeah, yeah. Fine."

"You're white as a sheet. You're not fine."

"It's nothing." He didn't know that I'd used my FireSoul power against the man who'd killed his friend Marin. That I'd stolen not only his secrets, but his Destroyer gift. I had to get a handle on it soon—and that meant practice—or I'd be in real trouble.

It'd only been two days, but the power was insistent. I had to learn to control it, or it would control me. The nausea was coming more often than it had been.

A bad freaking sign.

Fortunately, the nausea faded. I pulled away from Ares and shoved the hair off my face with my forearm, still clutching my conjured dagger. "Let's go. I don't want those roots to start up again." I pointed to the path twenty yards away. "Let's stay on the road."

Ares gave me a long look, but nodded. His suspicion was clear —and so was the promise of a thorough questioning later—but at least he'd let me go for now.

He stowed his blade in the ether with a quick flick of his wrist, then turned and walked toward the dirt road. I joined him, kicking the gray leaves as I walked, trying to see if any tree roots were at the surface.

None. They'd fully retreated.

We made it to the wide dirt path without incident. Once, it might have provided a roadway for wagons or other vehicles. But that was long ago. Leaves blew across the dirt, and the whole thing felt abandoned. At least the creepy black mist stayed off the road.

We walked side by side down the road. I kept my ears pricked for any sound and my other senses alert for danger. Though unease chilled my skin, along with the soft breeze, the forest was silent.

For now, at least.

"A *Burtnieki* is a Latvian wizard, isn't it?" I asked.

I'd read it in a book while sitting at the desk of Ancient Magic. At least, that was where I thought I'd learned it. That's how I learned most things, anyway.

"It is. Though the vampire realm exists in the ether, another realm, we're closest to the Baltic states. At least, our culture is."

"That's how you have your accent?"

"Yes. Not all vampires are from the Baltic states, but many are. My father was. My mother was Greek."

"Hence the name Ares."

"Exactly."

Something red flashed at the corner of my eye. I twisted, but it had disappeared. "Did you see that?"

"Something red?"

"Yeah."

"I caught a glimpse, but couldn't tell what it was."

"Weird." I didn't like unknown red things flying and lurking. I quickened my pace, glancing around as I walked. From the left, something caught my eye. I glanced over, just in time to see something large and red swoop through the trees. It was the size of a cow.

It shot high into the sky, too fast for me to make out any detail.

"They're big," I said, looking right. Another hovered high in the trees. "Birds?"

"No." Ares's eyes were wide with shock. "They're Pūķis."

"What the hell are Pūķis?"

But in that moment, one of the flying beasts swooped low and landed on the path with silent grace.

"Holy crap, that's a dragon!" I stepped back, my heart thundering.

The dragon was made of fire—red and orange and flickering brightly. Its onyx eyes watched me.

"You call this a Pūķi?" I asked.

"Yes. Another Latvian creature. But no one has seen one in centuries."

"Okay." I drew in a steady breath and stepped toward the Pūķi, who sat still, his head tilted as he studied me.

Ares shot out an arm to stop me, but I pushed it aside. "Don't stop me."

"Careful. They bite. Hard."

Slowly, I approached the Pūķi. Sitting on his haunches like this, he—or she—was taller than I was. Up close, I realized that I could see right through the beast's chest. The flame flickered and flared, but it wasn't solid. The dragon wasn't *on* fire. It *was* fire.

They weren't dragons in the traditional sense—those had died out long ago. But they were something like dragons.

Cass had some dragonet buddies that she'd found in Switzerland a few months ago. They showed up when she needed help. But they were the size of house cats.

This guy—he was big.

On instinct, I conjured an apple, then held it out to the Pūķi. The dragon leaned forward, sniffing delicately. Flame shot from its nostrils.

I laughed, jumping backward. The Pūķi huffed.

"Okay, okay." I stepped forward. "Don't burn me."

The creature leaned its neck forward and nipped the apple out of my palm. Though the flame of his muzzle brushed my palm, it felt only warm.

"How did you know to feed the Pūķi?" Ares asked.

I shrugged, conjuring another apple for a second fire dragon that had landed next to the first. "Everyone likes a snack."

"Especially Pūķis. Traditionally, they were house guardians and fed first at every meal."

I looked at the two Pūķi that sat in front of me. "You guys had a good situation for yourselves, huh?"

They just blinked, but I assumed they understood me.

"Why did they leave their houses?" I asked.

"No idea. No one knows. We thought they were all dead. But they like you."

I winked at the Pūķi. "It's mutual, fellas."

They huffed, a contented sound, and flame billowed from their noses. It blazed across my shirt. I jumped back, startled, but again, it didn't burn.

"That didn't hurt?" Ares asked.

"No."

"Strange. Their flesh can be touched, though it looks like fire. But the flame from their nostrils? That's actually fire."

"Well it didn't hurt me." I looked at the Pūķi. "Will you be our bodyguards?"

They blinked, then pushed off the ground and hovered overhead.

"You can take that as a yes," Ares said.

"Yeah." I grinned, looking up at my new buddies.

This. Was. Awesome.

We set off down the road again, my new buddies flying above.

"I could get used to this." I frowned. "But I suppose they can't leave this realm."

"No, they can't. But you can visit them, once you are an ally."

"So you think I'll pass the tests?"

His gaze cut to me, unreadable. "I hope so."

"Me too." The alternative *sucked*.

Suddenly, the Pūķis zipped ahead, hurtling down the path. They landed in the middle of the road, a hundred feet down. By the time we reached them, they'd spread their wings to create a wall.

"You don't want us to pass?" I asked.

They didn't move.

"That's a yes," Ares said.

"No kidding." I frowned at the Pūķis. "It's dangerous past there, isn't it?"

They didn't nod, but it was clear from their eyes that it was. I didn't know how I could read their intentions, but it was as natural as breathing.

"Well, I'm one badass bitch," I said to the Pūķis. "So don't worry about it. I've got to get to the volcano, and it's down the road." My dragon sense made that *very* clear. There was one way, and this was it. "But if you guys don't like it, you don't have to follow."

They huffed in unison, a sound of resignation, then took to the air. But they didn't fly away. Instead, they hovered over my head, flying along with us.

"It looks like you have your bodyguards," Ares said.

"Yeah, but I hope they'll be okay." I didn't like the idea of them going into a place that frightened them.

A hundred yards later, when a huge castle crested the horizon, it was clear what they were afraid of. The whole place was black, as if the stones and spires and flags had been covered in soot. Despite the bright light of the moon, it looked as if it were one with the dark night.

Behind it, a tall volcano jutted into the sky. It was peaked, made of black stone, and looked scary as hell. I was going *in* that thing?

I shuddered.

But first, I had to get through the castle.

"It looks like an evil fairytale castle," I said. "Nothing like the ones on earth."

"It didn't always look like this. I've seen pictures of it from before the *Burtnieki* moved in."

"He crapped it up, huh?"

Ares nodded.

The place had seven spires reaching high into the air. The

curtain wall was at least a hundred feet high, and the road led right up to a big gate. There were no roads around. Just dense forest.

"We can't go into the forest," I said. I could just *feel* it. In my heart and bones and muscles. That forest was dark, and it would kill us.

"We have to go through the castle?" Ares asked.

"Yeah."

"That sounds more dangerous. Are you sure?"

I glanced at him, studying his green eyes. "Is this a test? You know the way, right? As part of my trials?"

"I don't know everything. But through the castle seems like it's courting danger more than necessary."

I pointed to the black trees that surrounded the place. "Those are danger. The last trees that attacked us didn't even feel bad to me. But these? They're giving off a big *stay out.*"

"Do you have some kind of magic over plants?" Ares asked.

Surprise flared in my chest. "No." *Right?*

Something red caught my eye. It was hurtling from the castle, but it wasn't a Pūķi.

"Fire!" I dove left, rolling away as a fireball exploded into the ground where I'd been standing. Dirt flew into the air.

I scrambled up, turning. Ares had dived right and was surging to his feet.

"The *Burtnieki* knows we're here." He turned to the castle, squinting.

"Clearly. You sure you couldn't just transport us to the castle?"

"That's not part of the challenge."

"We could die."

"That's the point." His gaze was serious, brooking no argument.

Damn. I called upon my magic, conjuring a tall shield. I handed it off to Ares, then conjured my own. It was heavy, and wouldn't protect me from everything, but it was useful.

"Let's go." I set off down the path, trying to keep up an even pace while watching for more fireballs.

Ares ran at my side, his gaze alert on the castle.

Another fireball flew through the air, plowing into the ground right in front of us. I ducked behind my shield. Dirt sprayed up, clattering against the metal.

"Watch out! From the left!" Ares yelled.

I dove right instinctively. Another fireball hit the road where I'd been standing. While I'd been hiding, another fireball had been flying.

Shit.

I scrambled to my feet, racing forward. We dodged the fireballs. When we were about fifty yards away, I could make out a tall figure on one of the towers. His black cloak whipped in the wind, and his hands glowed with blue magic. The magic was the only reason I could see him—otherwise, he was camouflaged against the dark night.

He threw the blue light at us. It hurtled through the air, landing ten yards in front of us. The ground buckled, then rose up like a wave of dirt coming right at us.

CHAPTER FOUR

"Run!" I yelled. There was only one way through this, and that was over.

As I sprinted toward the wave of dirt, the two Pūķi hurtled toward the castle. I left them to it, focusing on the rocky ground beneath my feet.

Ares and I crested the wave of dirt, slipping and sliding as we sprinted. The ground was broken on the other side, a pit that plunged into the ground. It widened with every moment. Even now, it was four feet across.

"Jump!" Ares yelled.

I leapt, flying over the pit. My foot caught on the edge, but I lost my balance, pinwheeling my arms. Ares, who was so much taller, had no trouble landing on the other side.

He spun, his gaze stark with worry, and reached for me. His big hand gripped my arm, yanking me onto solid ground. I stumbled toward him.

"Come on!" He turned and sprinted for the castle gate, which was only thirty meters away now.

I ran after him, panting, my skin still cold from the fear of hanging over that pit of death. Had he been allowed to save me like that? Was that part of the rules?

I'd thought that if I died, no big deal to the Vampire Court.

I shook the thought from my head. I had no time for distractions.

High in the tower, the Pūķi were bombarding the wizard with blasts of fire from their snouts. He threw fire at them, but they absorbed it, growing bigger. So he changed tactics, hurling blue light instead—sonic booms, it sounded like. Though they tumbled through the air, they righted themselves quickly and returned for the attack.

They bought us enough time to reach the gate, which was a solid wooden affair painted black.

Ares turned to look at me, brow raised.

"My job, huh?" I asked.

"Your challenge."

"No problem." I leaned my shield against the gate, closed my eyes, envisioning the ingredients for dynamite, and conjured two sticks. If my calculations were right—and I'd studied hard so that they would be—this would be enough to take out the door but not the wall.

"Dynamite?" Ares asked as I conjured a match. "You sure about that?"

"I've done my research." I struck the match and lit the dynamite, then laid them at the base of the gate. "Come on."

I grabbed my shield, then sprinted twenty feet away and knelt behind the protection. Ares followed suit, looking at me.

"You've got guts," he said.

"Thanks." I grinned, waiting for the boom.

It didn't disappoint. Nor did the scream of rage that the wizard let loose.

I leapt to my feet. "We'd better hurry!"

I didn't know how long it would take the wizard to reach us, but I didn't want to find out. I raced through the burning rubble of the gate, entering a wide courtyard that was as black as the outside of the castle. The floor was dirt, and the torches on the walls were flickering with orange light.

"Creepy." I called on my dragon sense, seeking a way out of here. There had to be a gate on the other side. But I didn't want to go through the big building right in front of me. The main keep was four stories tall and radiated malevolence.

No wonder the goddess of fate hadn't wanted anything to do with this guy. If this was what was in his soul, it didn't matter how nice he was on the surface. Laima had sensed that.

"Which way?" Ares asked.

"I think we can go around." I dropped the shield, hoping for extra speed, and sprinted left, toward a dark alley between the main keep and another building that flanked it.

Whoever had built this place had filled the main compound full of stone buildings, but this would take us to the other side. I ran down the stone-paved corridor, Ares at my back. It was so dark in here, away from the light of the moon and torches, that I had to hold my hand out in front of me to make sure I didn't slam into anything.

In the distance, a red light glowed.

One of the Pūķi! It hovered at the exit of the alley, waiting for us. I raced faster, desperate to get out of the disgusting corridor and away from the mopey wizard with violent tendencies.

We spilled out into a back courtyard. Another gate loomed—smaller, but still big enough to cause a problem.

"Going to need more dynamite," Ares said.

The wizard yelled from somewhere in the castle, rage in his voice. He was getting closer. He had to be in the other courtyard, just a short run from us.

I began to conjure the dynamite, but the Pūķi who'd greeted us in the courtyard flew toward the gate, hurtling like a bomb.

He plowed into the door. It exploded outward, pieces of wood flaming.

Jackpot!

"Come on!" I cried.

We raced through the opening, onto a path identical to the one we'd left. Both Pūķis waited for us. I didn't hesitate—just kept running.

Ares stayed at my side, occasionally glancing back. When I looked over my shoulder, I saw the shadow of the wizard standing in the gateway. He wound up another one of his blue balls of magic.

"Sonic boom coming!" I yelled.

We sprinted faster. My heart thundered, and my lungs burned.

I *so* needed to work out more.

I could feel the sonic boom coming before it landed, like an energy in the air that prickled against my skin. When it hit the ground behind us, the force hurling me off my feet. I flew forward, throwing my arms out in front of me. Pain flared at my back, sharp and bright. Another burst of pain at my thigh.

I crashed into the ground, skidding on the dirt. Ares was at my side, in no better shape. The Pūķi slowed, turning to stare at us.

Pain sang through me as I scrambled up. A quick glance behind showed the wizard charging up another sonic boom.

I gasped. "Another one."

We ran. My leg blazed with every step. The next sonic boom took the wizard at least twenty seconds to charge up. By the time it hit the ground, we were far enough away that the blast only made me stumble.

I caught myself and kept running, my lungs burning.

Fates, this sucked. Give me a demon fight any day.

I couldn't remember ever being in a real school, but I'd have been shit at track and field.

The wizard's roar of rage pierced the air, making the hair

49

stand up on the back of my neck. But it was frustrated, too. As if we were out of his range.

I glanced back over my shoulder. It was almost impossible to see the wizard in the darkness. He had no magic blue ball to light him up.

"He's given up." I panted, stumbling to a walk. Holy crap, I needed a breather. Pain throbbed in my back and leg. I could not get a break with my leg these days.

Ares slowed beside me. "Are you all right?"

"Yeah." I twisted my torso, trying to figure out what was wrong with my back. "Did you get hit by anything?"

"Metal shards. I think they were in the sonic boom. A combo spell."

Freaking clever wizard.

Ares grabbed my arm, stopping me. "Let me check your back."

I wanted to say no, just to avoid the intimacy, but it hurt like the devil. "Fine."

I turned my back toward him. His hands were gentle as he moved my leather jacket. I assumed he was peeking at my wound. I heard him shift, then glanced behind to see him kneeling and checking out the gashes on the back of my thigh.

"They're deep," he said. "Let me heal them."

And make a greater connection to him through his vampire blood? Hell no. "Isn't that against the rules? Healing me?"

"I don't care."

Which meant it *was*. And he was going to break them. For me.

I stepped away, not wanting to think of what that meant. I wanted his trust—wanted his help. But him breaking the rules for me... That was a big deal.

I didn't like big deals.

Sure, I'd seen Del and Cass with their guys and thought that'd be pretty nice to have. Who wouldn't want a partner to stick by your side?

But Ares?

He was scary and dangerous and powerful. And he'd gotten me into this situation—these trials for my life. I didn't want to complicate things. Especially not by developing a growing bond with him through his blood.

"No." I turned to face him. He stood, meeting my gaze. "No rule breaking."

"I'm not going to watch you suffer."

Oh. Holy crap. His gaze was intense. I swallowed hard. "Fortunately, you don't have to." I dug into my pocket and pulled out the little vial. There wasn't much left, but it'd do the trick. I handed it to him. "If you could put just a bit of this on the wounds, it'd help."

He took it, studying the contents. "What is it?"

"A potion I made that has healing properties. It's rare." It'd taken me two years to track down the Arabena plant. The seeds were ancient, growing only in a small part of Croatia. Now, I was glad I'd made the effort. I turned, presenting him with my back. "Go on."

I heard the pop of the cork coming out of the vial, then felt my clothes rustle as he gently moved them. His hands were as light as a butterfly's wings on my back. For such a big guy, it was amazing how gentle he could be.

"It's going to take all the potion," he said.

I sighed. Since I could barely walk or twist my torso, it was necessary. "Fine."

The only pain came from the burn and sizzle of the potion. First on my back, then on my thigh. Knowing that Ares was so close made a weird shiver of pleasure race over my skin.

"This is impressive stuff," he said. "Your wounds healed almost instantly."

I turned to face him and held out my hand for the vial. It was empty, as he'd said. He passed it over.

"Could you make more of that?" he asked.

"Not much, and not quickly. It takes months for the plants to grow even a centimeter." It was why I so rarely used it. Twice in one day was unheard of. But desperate times and all.

"You're talented, Nix," he said.

"Thanks. I know."

He grinned. "Modest, too."

"Hey, I know my faults." I held up a hand, ticking them off on my fingers. "I'm crap at running, impulsive, drive too fast, eat too much cheese—my cholesterol must be terrible—and I'm a terrible writer. *But* I also know what I'm good at. I don't think people should downplay their accomplishments. No need to be a jerk about them, but…"

"I like that," he said.

"Thanks." I turned, starting down the path. "Now let's get a move on. That volcano waits for no woman."

It loomed tall overhead, a threat in the distance. We were probably only a mile away. It jutted straight out of the ground, like something from a fairy tale. Just like the castle.

"The Baltic doesn't have volcanos. But you guys do?" I asked.

"It also doesn't have giant trees with silver leaves. It's the magic. It manifests differently everywhere."

So of course it decided to manifest into a giant volcano that I would have to climb into. Fun!

We trekked toward the volcano, gradually ascending until we reached the true base. The rock was black and bare. There was no scrub brush or vegetation—just jagged stone climbing steeply up to form the mountain.

"Well, that looks delightful," I said.

Ares laughed.

I began to climb, scrambling over the steeper parts of the ascent. Some of the rocks were so sharp they cut my hands. I tried staying upright, but the mountain was so steep in places that it was impossible.

"Hang on." I stopped. Ares stopped beside me. I called upon

my magic, conjuring sturdy leather gloves, then tugged them on over my abused hands. I glanced at Ares. "Want some?"

He held out his hands, which were undamaged.

"You're just that good a climber, huh?" I asked.

He shrugged. "Not bad."

"Then onward." This time, my ascent was quicker. The stone couldn't cut my hands, so I placed them more quickly, scrambling up the mountain.

As I climbed higher, exhaustion began to pull at my limbs. Then a sharp pain bit into my calf. I yelped, looking downward. A dark gray tentacle had whipped out of the ground, sneaking from a crevice in the rock.

It had sharp, serrated edges that had bit into the muscle of my calf. I scrambled farther up a rock.

"What the hell is that?" I demanded.

"Mountain Laurel," Ares said.

"Uh, no. Mountain Laurel is a flower." I pointed to the tentacle, which was waving ominously. "That is a monster."

"It's a land squid." Ares climbed around the tentacle. "We call them Mountain Laurel."

"You vampires have a weird sense of humor."

He grinned. "Now move faster, or it will come out of its den."

"Righto." I gave it one last look, and climbed higher up the rock.

Unfortunately, another tentacle whipped out and sliced me across the arm. Pain flared and blood dripped down my sleeve. Ten feet away, another tentacle popped out. It was four feet long, and slowly inching out of the hole.

I did *not* want to see that guy's body.

All around, tentacles darted up out of the ground, waving in the air, their serrated edges gleaming in the moonlight.

Oh, shit.

Nightmare city.

The Pūķis, seeming to have realized how bad it had gotten,

joined us. They swooped and dived around me, blasting fire at the Mountain Laurel. Though they could hold off some, there were just too many.

I called upon my magic, conjuring a small shield. It'd have to do for now, because I couldn't manage a blade when I needed one hand to climb.

I looked at Ares. "Need one?"

He'd already conjured his shadow sword. "I'm good."

I nodded, then turned and climbed up the mountain. From left and right, the tentacles lashed out at me. Twenty yards up, a great black eye peered out of a little cave on the ground. A tentacle whipped out, straight for me.

I threw up my shield. The tentacle crashed into the metal, shoving me backward. I scrambled not to fall, then climbed higher up the mountain. At my side, Ares sliced off attacking limbs.

"They'll grow back," he said.

The higher we climbed, the worse the tentacles got. There were dozens, whipping out from beneath rocks. I could stop some, but others sliced into my arms and legs and back, leaving shallow, painful wounds.

Every inch of me was on fire.

I gasped. "Are these tentacles poisonous?"

"Not to vampires." Ares grunted and sliced at another.

Considering I wasn't a vamp, I must be allergic, or something. Because the wounds burned and itched. My head swam as I climbed higher, my lungs heaving. Gradually, my vision grew blurry.

The top of the mountain still loomed far ahead. Beside me, Ares was dripping blood from many shallow wounds. Though he was faster than me, he seemed determined to stick by my side.

Out of solidarity, or because of his Vampire Court duties?

"You're faster than this," I gasped. "You should go ahead."

"I'll be fine. I heal."

I opened my mouth to say something, but another tentacle swatted out. It took everything I had to repel the attack. Soon, I had no breath left for anything except scrambling up the mountain, fighting off tentacles. The Pūķis swooped and dived around us, lighting up the Mountain Laurel as fast as they could.

Shit, this was hard.

In normal life, my conjuring magic and mean right hook got me as far as I needed. Thieves didn't stand a chance when they stepped foot inside Ancient Magic.

But this? Magical challenges and weirdo monsters with serrated tentacles?

I was out of my league.

Maybe I did need more magic than just the conjuring.

I shoved the thoughts aside and focused on the task, fighting and clawing my way to the top of the mountain, breath heaving as my vision blurred. My muscles felt like jello, propelled only by my desire to reach the top. Soon, I felt like a machine, my dumb body obeying the command of my mind.

By the time I reached the top of the volcano, right at the lip where it dropped down into the depths of the earth, my vision had darkened at the edges. Blood slicked my skin and dripped down my neck from a particularly deep gash. The Pūķis sat a dozen yards away, gazing into the volcano with delight. Ares stood next to me, his chest heaving.

Fortunately, there were no more tentacles this far up the mountain.

And good thing, too. Because from the look of Ares and the way I felt, we weren't up for another fight.

"How are you?" Ares voice was rough as he reached for my hand, tugging me into the shelter of some large rocks.

Only then did I realize that a chilly wind was cutting across the top of the volcano, drying the blood on my skin. Despite the heat that bellowed out, the wind cut coldly through it. I shivered, stepping into the shelter of the stone, close to Ares.

More blood gleamed red in the moonlight, stark against Ares's pale cheek. It soaked his shirt and covered his hands. I looked down at myself. Blood coated cartoon Maru and his box, a gruesome sight.

"We look like shit." I swayed on my feet, blinking at Ares.

Though hazy vision, I saw the cut on his cheek stop bleeding. I squinted, watching the very edges of the wound knit closed.

"Amazing," I murmured.

"My healing is particularly powerful." He glanced around me, out at the night.

"Looking for something?" My words slurred. Shit, this was bad. Blood loss and maybe even the tentacle's poison were really getting to me.

"No."

Lie. But I didn't have the strength to call him out on it.

He met my gaze. "You need my help to heal."

"No!" I stepped back, stumbling. I was so clumsy now! Damned tentacles. "I don't... don't want your blood."

"Do you want to finish this challenge or do you want to die on this mountaintop?" Ares asked. "You'll fail."

Fail. I shuddered, hating the word.

"Nix, I've never seen anyone so underprepared for a Vampire Court challenge in my life."

"Heyyyy...." I slurred.

But he was right.

"You're the bravest, most determined person I've ever seen." His gaze was fierce, made even more so by the vampire change that this place induced. "You clawed your way up that mountain when you should have died from the poison a hundred yards back."

"Not a...quitter."

"No, clearly. But conjuring will only get you so far. And you don't have the magic for this. Your strength has gotten you to this point, but you need more."

Fates, he was right. I could hardly see now. My muscles were giving out. Every inch of my skin felt like it was on fire.

I *was* going to fail.

I might rule the roost back at Ancient Magic, but here I was only a chicken. And I was about to get my neck wrung.

CHAPTER FIVE

"Fine," I slurred.

I needed all the help I could get, especially now that my healing potion was gone. My *deirfiúr* did this stuff all the time, and I helped them out. But I was always the sidekick, never the leader.

I didn't have the magic to be the leader, but at least I could have the strength. The determination.

So whatever side effects there were from his blood... I was just going to have to deal with them.

"Just a little." I pointed to my neck, at the gash I felt was the deepest. Last time, he'd smeared a bit of his blood on a wound and the flesh had knitted back together. "Heal that one."

"Not that way. The poison is your problem." He lifted his right wrist, pulling back his sleeve and wiping the dirt and blood away with the bottom of his shirt.

"What are you—" I had to reach out, grabbing onto his strong shoulder to steady myself. Woo boy, this blood loss—or poison or whatever—was a real doozy.

Ares raised his wrist to his mouth, parting his lips to reveal his white fangs. The two incisors—the biters, as I thought of them—were slightly extended and gleaming white.

My breath caught in my throat as I watched his fangs puncture his flesh. Something warmed inside. Pleasant, but really weird.

I was a weirdo for liking that.

I blinked, trying to clear my hazy vision, as Ares raised his wrist to my lips.

"What—what—" I shook my head, stepping back.

But his other arm reached up, gently grasping my bicep and holding me still.

"Drink. Just a little."

"Hell no!" *Drink!?*

"It won't turn you into a vampire, you know that."

Yeah, the only way to make vampires was the old-fashioned way. I swallowed hard.

Omygodomygodomygod. Was I really going to do this?

"It's your only shot, Nix. You need the strength to get into the volcano. The poison is shutting down your organs and you won't have me to help you. I leave after this."

I nodded dumbly, my survival-based lizard brain having already decided what I would do.

I would *not* die on this mountaintop.

Tentatively, as my mind shrieked in utter shock at the gross thing I was about to do, I darted out my tongue to swipe at the dark blood pearling on his pale skin.

The first taste electrified me. Strength and light and pleasure exploded through my body, going from my mouth down through every inch of flesh and blood and bone.

Ares's lids dropped low as he watched me. His eyes burned, hot and fierce. The sharp cut of his cheekbones was like glass, the muscles of his neck corded.

My gaze darted down. It was too intimate. Though the pleasure surged through me, making me woozy in a good way, I had enough sense not to make this too crazy.

Correction, I *barely* had enough sense.

But what I had, I clung to. I just needed enough strength to get into that volcano. Not enough to jump his bones.

I took one more swipe of his blood, eyes rolling back in my head at the divine taste, then stepped back.

My feet were more steady, my muscles strong. The fogginess in my head was from residual pleasure, not poison. Even my thoughts were quicker.

"My blood will continue to work, strengthening you," he said.

"I've had enough?" Please say yes. Because a no….

I probably *would* jump his bones.

And frankly, that was a *bad* freaking idea.

"I think so." He gestured behind me, to the mouth of the volcano. "This is where I must leave you. From here, the challenge must be completed on your own."

"And if I bite it?"

His gaze darkened. "There is nothing I can do."

From the tone of his voice, he did *not* like that.

"Right." I saluted. "Thanks for the pick-me-up."

And I really did feel better. Eight percent and increasing. I spun and hurried away from the rock enclosure, realizing too late that he probably hadn't been getting out of the wind.

He'd been getting away from prying eyes.

That meant that Magisteria and Doyen must be up here somewhere, watching to see how I fared at the end of the challenge.

It was against the rules to heal me. And he'd broken them.

As least he was one of the three rulers, but still…

Going against the other two was risky. Though Ares had never struck me as the kind of guy to be frightened of going against the grain.

I glanced back over my shoulder. He stood, the rocks at his

back framing him, and watched me. With the blood streaking his skin and clothes, he looked like some kind of monster.

In a way, he was.

A vampire.

But not a bad one. Right?

I turned back, focusing on my footing. The rocks were uneven leading up to the mouth of the volcano. Nearby, the Pūķi sat, staring into the pit. Excitement flowed off of them, an energy that electrified me.

The fire dragons loved the volcano. No surprise.

Together, they looked up at me, their eyes bright.

"Having fun?"

They didn't nod, but it was clear. They were loving this.

Me? Not so much.

I stepped up to the rim of the volcano, looking down.

Holy fates.

The pit extended hundreds of meters deep. At the bottom, lava glowed bright red.

I had to go in there? I knew it, but I couldn't help but pray for an alternative.

My dragon sense tugged hard, indicating *Yes.*

Damn it.

I squinted, studying the inside of the volcano. Moonlight didn't provide much illumination, especially not down there, but a dark spot seemed to float in the middle.

An island or a jut of rock? Probably.

Only one way to know for sure.

I scouted the walls of the pit for a way down. They weren't entirely vertical. Instead, they sloped down steeply, black jagged rock providing meagre footholds.

Oh, this was going to be a *blast.*

I sucked in a ragged breath. I was still wearing the gloves, so this was about as good as it was going to get for me. After studying the volcano for a while, I found the best route.

As least, I hoped it would be.

I saluted the Pūḳi. "Wish me luck, fellas."

They blew a bit of fire out their noses, which I chose to interpret as their greatest well wishes. I turned back to the volcano.

Okay. Time to climb into this insane thing.

I didn't turn around to look at Ares one last time. Now was the time for action, not distraction. Carefully, I made my way along the edge of the volcano's mouth to the path that I'd spotted.

It was steep and narrow, more a natural groove carved by rainwater, but it was enough to get me started. I climbed down, alternating crab walking and crawling. Soon, my thighs burned from crouching and my biceps from clinging on. The walls had to be a seventy-degree angle, at least. Enough that I'd tumble into the lava if I lost my footing.

It was dark and hard to see, but my eyes adjusted to the light provided by the moon.

It took ages to climb down, and the farther I went, the hotter it got. Sweat dripped off every inch of me and my muscles burned from strain. I was only halfway to the bottom when a rumbling noise sounded from above. I glanced up, just in time to see a boulder hurtling toward me.

Shit!

I leapt out of the way, clinging to the side of the path. The boulder rumbled past me, inches from my fingertips. I scrambled, trying to find a toehold to push myself back onto the narrow path.

Finally, I made it, gasping and panting. I clung to the rock for a moment, trying to get my trembling muscles to calm, then continued down. Rocks dug into my stomach and sides and I crawled down the wall. It was no longer a graceful climb—I was just clinging for my life, trying to reach the bottom.

The heat was immense, a cloying thickness that filled my lungs. Sweat dripped down my face and into my eyes, searing them. Suddenly, I was starving, as if the strain had eaten away my insides.

I chanced a glance behind me, catching sight of the Pūķi diving into the lava that was fifty meters below. They loved it, swirling and swimming. It glowed orange and red, the same color as they.

Terrifying.

Dread curdled in my stomach as I took in the scene.

Shit.

With all the black rock and red lava, it was like that scene in Star Wars, where a young Darth Vader met his horrible fate. It had looked too terrible to be real in the movie. And yep—it was terrible.

By the time I stumbled onto the strip of flat ground at the bottom, every muscle I had burned like it was on fire. Hunger gnawed at my belly and my eyes watered.

I crept toward the edge of the rock platform, looking down into the depths. Forty feet below the lip of rock where I stood, glowing lava bubbled and surged. Across from me, a flat black island stood surrounded by the bubbling lava. Like a horrible moat.

The heat was insane. Thank fates I'd had some of Ares's blood. I wouldn't have stood a chance otherwise.

Though the lava was forty feet below, the heat made my skin feel like it was burning.

I squinted at the dark island, noticing a lump.

What the heck?

I tilted my head, peering through the heat waves wafting off the lava below.

Holy fates! That was a body!

A person was on that island!

Adrenaline surged through me, leaving my limbs shaky but clearing my mind.

I had to get to them. They needed help.

Frantically, I glanced around, searching for a way across. Of course, there was none. I hadn't seen any bridges when I'd had my bird's eye view up top, and from down here there was nothing but a lava lake surrounding the island.

The Pūki were still diving and pirouetting in the air. They were so ephemeral I didn't think I could ride them. They were the size of cows, but their bodies were slender and not fully solid.

But maybe they could help me?

I just needed a way across. It was about twenty feet to the island.

A jet pack would come in super handy right about now, but no way I could conjure something that complicated. And there was no wind for a hang glider.

A bridge, though… That, I could do. Especially if the Pūki helped me. They could eat apples, which meant they could influence the physical world. Hopefully they'd be strong enough for this.

I called upon my magic, conjuring a thick wooden board coated in a layer of adobe, the clay that could withstand great heat. Hopefully it wouldn't melt. The thing was twenty-five feet long and two feet wide.

If I could have conjured it right over the lava, that would have been ideal—but that kind of spacial control was beyond me. Whatever I conjured normally just ended up sitting smack in front of me.

Which was how the wood and adobe board appeared. I panted from the exertion of conjuring such a large object, my strength sapped. It'd have to do.

"Hey guys! A little help here!" I called.

The Pūkis looked up, then flew over. Their curious gazes were glued to me as I crouched down and pushed the board toward the edge of the stone platform. I lined it up so the narrow end would extend out toward the island, like a bridge.

I pointed toward the end. "I need you guys to support it from underneath as I push."

Please understand. Please be capable.

I had no idea if this was within their strength. But I pushed my makeshift bridge, straining and sweating and swearing.

And praying.

Please fates. A little help right now. My muscles were jello and my magic was severely depleted. I didn't have many more options.

The Pūķis seemed to figure it out, diving low to support the thing with the tops of their heads. They fluttered along, helping me guide my bridge to the little island.

Sweat rolled down my temples, down my forehead, down my back. Everywhere.

Finally, through burning eyes, I saw the edge of the bridge connect with the island. I pushed a couple more feet so it sat sturdily, then collapsed to my side, gasping.

The heat was *really* getting to me.

"No time to wimp out." That guy needed me.

I heaved myself up and started across the bridge, running as fast as I dared. Fear cloaked my hot skin in ice, making my stomach lurch. I chanced a peek below me at the lava that boiled and bubbled.

Oh, hell no.

This was insane. The heat was off the charts—unlike anything I'd ever felt. Far worse than on the other side of the bridge. The safe side, as I laughingly thought of it.

My thighs trembled as I ran across, trying desperately to maintain my footing. When I finally made it to the other side, I stumbled to my knees. I wanted to stay here, panting, but forced myself to crawl toward the lump that I was certain was a person.

It was.

A man, about thirty years old with sallow skin and mouse brown hair, lay on his back. Sweat shined on his skin. My breath heaved as I scrambled to find his pulse. It fluttered, weak but steady, against my fingertips.

What the hell?

I studied him, noting that an iron shackle bound his ankle to the stone.

What the hell did any of this have to do with gold?

At the thought, my dragon sense perked up, tugged me toward the man. I stumbled back onto my butt.

Oh, hell no.

But my dragon sense roared, pulled me to him. Igniting a hunger in my belly that was a thousand times worse than anything I'd felt when I'd started climbing into this volcano.

I reached out with my sense, feeling for his signature. I got a hit of something familiar. Something that Cass possessed.

A transporter!

Maybe he could get us out of here—because there was no way I had the strength to climb back out. But there was something else, too. I focused, trying to figure out what his other signature was. Through eyes cloudy with sweat, I saw that he glowed a bright gold, his aura a glittering mass of yellow light.

Shit. An alchemist.

Oh, shit.

No. No. No.

These monsters—Magisteria and Doyen and even Ares—wanted me to steal this man's gift.

It was the only reason.

They didn't want me to rescue him. This was no normal trap. He'd been put here by them. So that I could kill him and steal his magic as part of my test. They wanted me to do a horrible thing.

The problem was, so did my FireSoul. It clawed and screamed inside of me, desperate to get out. Shaking, I stumbled away.

I'd never felt hunger like this—a ravenous desire to use my gift to steal. But I'd never been confronted with an alchemist before. Of course my FireSoul would love to possess the power to turn anything into gold.

It was the heart of a dragon. And I was a dragon.

And I needed more power. I'd been so weak getting here. My magic had helped, but not enough. Without Ares's healing power, I'd never have made it.

It was clear I needed more power.

This man's power.

No!

"I can't!" I cried. "I won't."

The air in front of me shimmered, white and glowing. Soon, Doyen appeared, her red hair gleaming even brighter in the glow of the lava. Her white robe glowed brightly, so clean and pure. Like her.

My brain stuttered. That thought was weird. She was far from pure.

"You must, Phoenix Knight." Her voice sang with power. "Take this man's power. He is evil. He deserves it."

I looked down at the man. He was still unconscious, but she was right—even like this, he looked evil.

He was a *bad* man. My mind was cloudy, but that thought was obvious. This dude was bad news. I could take his power and not feel guilty.

"Do it, Phoenix. And you will join us."

Hunger gnawed at my belly as I looked back and forth between Doyen and the man.

"You could use his power. Become even stronger." Her eyes blazed with power. Her magic rolled off of her.

She was right. My gaze darted to him, then back to her. Something in her gaze gleamed.

I blinked, shaking my head. Some of the fogginess in my mind dissipated. I shook my head again, trying to drive the rest away.

"You're screwing with my mind," I said. Her gift was mind

control. She was trying to make me think this man was evil. To make me kill him. "You snake."

I crawled toward the man, putting my hand on his head. "I feel no dark magic on him."

Doyen turned to face me, glaring down. "He doesn't need dark magic to be evil."

"That's true. But I have no reason to trust you." Fates, I was hot. My head was swimming, my FireSoul gnawing at my belly.

I used my magic to conjure a gallon of water, chugging some of it, then splashing it on the man. He didn't wake, but I felt a bit more sensible.

I needed to embrace my magic—and yes, I needed more of it —but not like this. Not from an innocent man.

It was too much like my past. Too much like my time in the Monster's dungeon.

And Doyen was too much like him.

I spat at her. "Fuck you, Doyen. I'm not your dog. You want me to take his alchemy and make gold for you, is that it? He won't do it?"

She tilted her head. I took it to be a yes.

"Well I won't either. I'm not killing him." I stood, stepping away, toward my bridge. I had no freaking idea how I was going to have the strength to get out of here, but I needed to find it. "You put that poor bastard here, you get him out. Ask him nicely to make your gold. I hear that works wonders. Maybe even try the word *please*."

"We will *not*." Doyen's voice was so cold I swore it sent a lovely chill breeze through this nightmare volcano.

I turned to her. "Won't ask nicely or won't get him out of here?"

"We will not take him."

Truth.

So much truth in her voice.

"So he'll die either way, is that it?" I asked. "You sweeten the deal, telling me he's as good as dead?"

"You can't get him out of here. So if you leave, he will die. If you take his power, he will die. But at least you will have his power."

Rage filled me. At her doubt. At her cunning plan. At my odds of failure. I sucked in a breath, using it to fuel my determination.

"You think I can't do it?" I demanded.

"Of course you can't. You could barely get yourself down here. I doubt you'll make it out alive. Much less with him."

"You're gonna eat those words." Because I wouldn't let that man die. I wouldn't let this bitch win. And I certainly wouldn't spend my last hours on earth sucking in this boiling hot air and sweating like a fireman.

I didn't have the strength—she was right. But I was no flipping quitter. I'd trick my own body if I had to. We were getting the hell out of here.

I didn't know how, but I'd figure it the frick out.

CHAPTER SIX

I stumbled toward the man, landing heavily on my knees next to him. The heat was really getting to me on this nightmare island.

It'd already gotten to him, from the look of things. Sweat soaked his clothes and coated his skin. I'd have to get some water into him, try to revive him, but first I needed to get him off this island.

This heat would never allow him to wake. At least the ledge on the other side was a bit cooler. I still didn't know how we were getting there, but I'd figure it out.

One step at a time.

I'd once heard a saying: Inch by inch, life is a cinch, yard by yard, life is hard.

Well, I'd be going by fractions of an inch, but I'd get there.

"Quit staring at me," I said to Doyen as I inspected the shackle at the man's ankle. I could feel her gaze on my back.

The shackle was a simple, old style—but made of solid iron. That meant no breaking out of it. But breaking into it?

That, I could do.

I conjured some little picks for the lock and set to work, slipping the two slender pieces of metal into the hole where the key would go. It took a few moments, mostly me being clumsy because of my exhaustion, but finally, the locks nicked.

"Jackpot." I tugged the metal off his ankle.

"Hardly," Doyen sneered. "You're so weak you can barely keep yourself upright. You have basically no magic. That man weighs more than you do. No way you can carry him out of here."

I studied the man, grateful to see that he wasn't that much bigger than me. One hundred and sixty pounds, max. And only five ten.

"I've got this." I stood, mind racing. I had to get him to the other side.

How?

I didn't have much magic left. Exhaustion was dragging at me. I studied my narrow bridge. An idea popped into my mind, simple and terrifying.

But I didn't waste any time debating. I didn't have time to waste. Not down here. Now when my bridge wouldn't last forever and my strength was on its way out.

So I called upon my magic, conjuring a big wheelbarrow with a wooden wheel. Rubber wouldn't work down here. I laughed when it appeared, realizing how insane my idea was.

And how I had no other options.

"Are you serious?" Doyen demanded.

"As a heart attack." My own heart pounded as I tried to heave the man into the wheelbarrow.

This was utterly insane.

But I kept going, straining to heave his bulk into my repurposed gardening tool. When I finally got him in, my breath was heaving.

He looked like a rag doll, or a drunken dude being wheeled home from the pub.

I wished I were wheeling him home from a pub.

Instead, I was about to wheel him across some lava while my muscles screamed and my head swam. I pushed him toward the narrow bridge. I could really use one of those lava suits right about now, but I was almost completely drained.

It wasn't going to happen.

"That is insane." Shock and awe colored Doyen's voice.

"I completely agree." I sucked in a bracing breath, then pushed the wheelbarrow onto the bridge.

I had to force myself to breathe as I balanced the wheelbarrow and myself. Speed was key to balancing a wheelbarrow—I knew that from my garden trove—so I pretended I was pushing a load of dirt on a sunny day and headed straight for the other side.

The heat warmed my boots and made sweat pour into my eyes—I didn't think they'd ever stop burning—but I kept going, trying to outrun the heat that dragged at my every step.

Inside my head, a stranger shrieked with insane laughter at the situation. It felt like I was two people—the insane person pushing a wheelbarrow over lava and a rational person marveling at the lunacy. An out-of-body experience.

Through the haze, I heard a popping sound from behind me. I glanced back, seeing some of the adobe pop off the wooden bridge, propelled by steam from inside the wood.

Shit.

My bridge was faltering. The wood must have been a bit wet. The result…

Disaster.

Bits of adobe popped off the bridge left and right as the water in the wood turned to steam. My heart thundered in my ears as I picked up the pace, sprinting. Trying to outrun my breaking bridge.

It wobbled beneath me. I almost lost my balance, catching myself and the wheelbarrow at the last minute.

The man slept through it all, limp body dangling precariously over bubbling lava.

I sucked in a ragged breath of steamy air and hurtled the last three feet, making it onto solid ground as the bridge behind me exploded in a mass of steam and flying adobe and wood.

I dived to the ground, covering my head. A shard of adobe sliced my ear, the pain sharp. I stayed there for a moment, huddling against the ground and hoping it was over.

When I stood and turned to the lava, the bridge was gone.

Shit.

My knees gave out and I collapsed, catching myself on my hands. I gave myself two seconds—two blissful seconds—of pretending this was over, then I climbed up and sneered at Doyen, who watched me.

I didn't wait for her response, just turned back to my wheelbarrow to see my new buddy still passed out cold.

I approached and gripped the wheelbarrow handles, then pushed the man farther to the edge, near the wall of the volcano. As I'd hoped, it was cooler a bit farther from the lava.

It was still terrible over here, but much cooler. Unable to control my shaking legs and desperately needing some water, I sank to my butt and leaned against the wheelbarrow.

"We made it, pal." I conjured a jug of water and gulped, replacing the quarts that I'd lost to sweat.

Quenched, I struggled to my feet and turned to him, then poured the water on his head.

I swear to fates, his head sizzled.

Honestly, it looked delightful. If I had a moment to spare, I'd have poured some on me too. Instead, I lifted his head and tried pouring it into his mouth.

It burbled out of his lips, dribbling down his chin.

I looked up at the exit to the volcano, three hundred yards above us. Maybe more. The moon hung right overhead, a bright beacon that was so damned far away.

"We're screwed, dude." I looked back down at him.

His eyes were fluttering open!

I shook his shoulder. "Come on, you gotta wake up!" I poured a thin stream of water over his lips. He shuddered, then drank. "That's it. Drink up."

He drank at least a quarter of the gallon, then opened his eyes.

He sure didn't look evil. I glared at Doyen, who still stood on the island, watching me, then glanced back at the man.

"You gotta get up. Can you transport us?" *Please, please, please.*

"I—" he coughed, shaking his head. "Too weak."

"We'll die in here." I pulled at him, trying to get him to stand. He managed it, barely. For just a moment. Then his legs wobbled and he collapsed against me.

Shit.

"Come on, pal." I shook him.

He managed to straighten, his pale blue gaze meeting mine. In his khaki pants and collared shirt, he looked like a bank manager on the weekend. One who'd spent Saturday in a volcano.

"Where are we?" he asked.

"In a volcano."

He swallowed hard, his Adam's apple bobbing, then looked around. His eyes widened until I could see white all around the irises. He gulped in air like a fish.

I gripped his collar. "Focus. You want to live, you have to focus."

Like a man who suddenly understood it was do or die—which it was—he sucked in a ragged breath and his features calmed. He nodded.

"Can you transport us?" I asked. "Or even just yourself?"

He shook his head, despair in his blue eyes. "I'm a weak transporter. Can barely manage across a room on good days."

Disappointment filled my chest. Felt like I'd eaten rocks.

I'd bet he was a good alchemist, dang it. Something completely useless in this scenario.

I glanced up, hoping to see Ares coming to help.

There was no Ares.

Damn it.

I looked back at the man. "What's your name?"

"Kevin."

"Okay, Kevin. We're climbing out of here."

He looked up at the volcano walls, brows up to his hairline. "How? The wall is vertical!"

"That's a seventy-degree angle. Ain't nothin." *Oh my fates, we'd never make it.* I pasted on an encouraging smile. "It's literally climb or die, pal. And I choose climb."

He nodded, head wobbly.

I was going to scale a nearly vertical wall with a bobblehead doll.

This was gonna be great.

And we might not survive it. It'd been hard enough to make it down. That'd been before I'd conjured a giant bridge and crossed some lava. My muscles felt like spaghetti and exhaustion pulled at my mind. My magic was shot.

Better get to it, then. I studied the wall, looking for our best path out. Same as the way in, it looked like. I pointed up. "We'll go up that way."

He swallowed hard, then nodded.

I looked back at Doyen, who stood, watching us. I glanced at Kevin. "How did they capture you?"

I wanted to know how evil they really were. Would they try to stop us from climbing out?

"I was at work. At the bank." He rubbed a hand over his face.

Bingo on the bank.

"One minute I was in the back, putting some papers away in the office, and the next, I was here. They must have made me sleep, or something."

"Hmmm." That wasn't too brutal, at least. I used the very last of my magic to conjure another pair of gloves and handed them to Kevin. "Put these on. The rock is sharp."

He tugged them on.

I gave Doyen a last glare, then turned to the rock wall. "Let's go. I'll lead the way—you put your feet where I put mine."

"All right." His voice barely wavered.

I had to give it to the guy—he might look skinny and frail, but he was tough. One minute he's a banker, the next he's climbing out of a volcano.

I began to climb, focusing all my energy on picking the perfect foothold. It was rough going, and my feet slipped out from under me a few times.

"How you holding up?" I called over my shoulder.

"I—I—" Kevin was so out of breath he couldn't talk.

"Just keep climbing." I grabbed a little ledge and pulled myself up, muscles trembling like a bowl of wobbly jello.

Out of the corner of my eye, I caught sight of one of the Pūķis, swooping through the air. They were keeping their eye on us, I liked to imagine.

My muscles screamed as I climbed, weakening with every foot I ascended. Behind me, Kevin was breathing so heavily I thought he might have a heart attack.

And we were still only halfway there.

My foot slipped and my weight dragged me down. Kevin shouted. I clung to the rock, on such a steep slope that I'd slide all the way down if I lost my footing.

"Help!" Kevin's voice sounded from behind me.

I glanced down.

He clung to the rock, same as me. My fall must have startled him, triggering his own. I tried to pull myself up, my feet scrambling for purchase.

But I was too weak—from the conjuring, the injuries, the heat. I was a car with no gas in the middle of the desert.

Chills raced over my skin.

"Kevin!" I gasped. "You can do this."

"I can't!" he cried.

The desperation in his voice mirrored what was in my heart.

We were screwed.

I strained, pulling myself up only inches as my heart thundered in my chest and my stomach hollowed out in fear.

Help!

But I didn't know who I was calling to.

A Pūķi flashed by me, then something warm pressed against my butt and legs, pushing me upward. I glanced back.

The Pūķi was giving me a boost! And the other was helping Kevin. I prayed they didn't breathe fire on poor Kevin. But they were our only shot.

I pulled, giving it the last of my strength, scrambling onto a slightly better bit of rock.

"Thank you!" I gasped. The Pūķi couldn't fly me up, but he was strong enough for a push.

Kevin clung to a little ledge below me. I met his wide gaze. "We can do this. The Pūķis will help us."

He nodded, his head bobbing. There was determination in his gaze. And hope. With dragons on our side—even small ones like the Pūķi—we really had a chance.

We continued our scrambling climb up the mountain, the Pūķi helping to push us up, and the reality of my situation hit me. I almost laughed. I was climbing out of a volcano—one filled with lava, no less—with a Latvian dragon spirit pushing me by the rear.

Every inch of my body sang with pain, but I kept going, the Pūķi's spirit giving me strength as much as his pushing.

By the time I scrambled out onto the rim of the volcano, I was dripping sweat and trembling like a dog in a thunderstorm.

Kevin flopped up beside me. A quick glance showed that he was in no better shape, his hair matted with sweat and his eyes wide.

"Sorry about this, Kev," I said. "They wouldn't have captured you if not for me."

He gave a wobbly grin. "As long as I get out of here, I don't care. Don't get many adventures like this, working in a bank."

I laughed, gasping for breath. "No one gets adventures like this."

The Pūķi who'd helped me flew around to land in front of my head. He peered down, his head close to mine and black eyes peering curiously at me.

I patted him gently on the nose. "Thanks, pal. You saved our bacon."

Fire ruffled from his nose, a tickle against my skin. His buddy landed next to him. I used the last of my strength—praying I wouldn't need it for anything else—and conjured two apples, handing one to each dragon.

"Dragons. They like you," Kevin's eyes were wide at the sight of the dragons.

"We're pals." I staggered to my feet, my hand on one of the Pūķi's shoulders for strength.

Ares appeared at the corner of my vision, having approached from his viewing point, no doubt.

"Fat lot of help you were," I muttered.

In the cold light of the moon and the warm light of the volcano, his face was a contrast between the more human Ares that I'd met in Magic's Bend, and the vampiric one who'd appeared as soon as we'd stepped foot in his realm.

The vampire realm definitely did something to him.

"You did well," he said.

Magisteria and Doyen appeared next to him. Doyen had transported herself out of the volcano, but I wasn't sure where Magisteria had been hanging out. No doubt lurking like a spider to see if I fell in some lava.

I scowled at the three of them.

Kevin stepped slightly behind me. I couldn't blame him. At least *I'd* known I'd be getting myself into some serious shit with these folks. He'd just been doing paperwork at some bank.

"You did well." Magisteria inclined her head so slightly I might have imagined it.

"Yes. You passed," Doyen said.

Annoyance surged, filling my veins with temporary strength. "Are you freaking serious?" I pointed to Kevin. "You wanted me to steal from this guy! You put me through mental hell to do it! You put *him* through hell!"

"That was the test," Ares said. "We want an ally, not a minion. You showed moral fortitude and that you can't be swayed from the path of right. Not even by threat of death or being revealed."

"Well I coulda told you that!" I threw up my hands. "I've lived a life not abusing my power. But you guys had to put me through hell—muck around inside my mind, manipulating my thoughts—in order to figure it out?" *That's* what really got me. I didn't mind the physical challenges. Didn't love it, but whatever. The mind manipulation, though? Putting Kevin in danger?

Screw that.

"It was the best way," Doyen said.

"Whatever, screw you." I swayed on my feet, exhausted beyond reason, then turned to Kevin. "You want to get out of here?"

He nodded, but his face was so pale I could almost see the veins beneath his skin. A moment later, his eyes rolled back in his head and he passed out. The Pūki nearest him shifted to break his fall, but Kevin was sprawled out on the rocks a moment later.

I knelt, checking his pulse. Alive. Out cold, was all.

I stood and turned to the vampires. "I cannot believe you guys. You're the worst."

Doyen and Magisteria's eyes flared. Ares gave a slight grin.

"No one speaks to us like that." Magisteria's voice was cold.

Fear shivered across my skin, but I propped my hands on my hips, going for bold. "Well, maybe it's time someone did. You've clearly forgotten what decency means."

They ignored my brashness, but I'd take it. Better than them

79

smiting me for my insolence. I could barely stand, much less fend off a vampire attack.

"We will return Kevin to his home." Doyen stepped forward, her eyes on the prone man. "His role is done here."

Again, I believed her. Same as when she'd said she'd leave Kevin in the volcano, she meant this. Probably because he was a pawn and his use was over. Cleaning up the trash, in her mind, I'd bet.

"Good." I knelt by Kevin and fished around for his wallet, pulling it out of his pocket and finding his ID. Kevin Michaels. 12 Fortitude Lane, Magic's Bend. Address memorized—no wonder he lived on Fortitude Lane, because that dude had some—I put everything back in his pocket. I stood and met Doyen and Magisteria's gazes. "I know who he is and where he lives. If he's not there tomorrow, I'm coming for you."

Doyen and Magisteria scoffed, but I turned from them. I avoided Ares's gaze, not liking the vampire version of him. "I'm getting out of here. Let me know when the next challenge is."

I turned, stomping off across the lip of the volcano. At least, I tried to stomp. It was more of a stumble. I was getting out of here even if it meant fighting my way back through that miserable wizard's freaking castle and the poisonous Mountain Laurel tentacles.

I was about twenty yards away, out of sight of the vampires, when Ares joined me. Whether that was good or bad, I had yet to determine.

"Let me help you get out of here," he said.

"*Now* you can help?" I kept walking, dreading the poison tentacles that weren't far away now.

"You handled yourself well back there," he said.

"Yeah. That was the point, wasn't it? To prove myself?"

"You did a good job."

"Thanks. But I don't like tricks. Or mind games."

"Vampires love them."

I turned to him. "I got that impression." I poked him in the chest. "But if you think of pulling any of that mind-game shit with me, you're going to regret it."

"That's not my gift. It's Doyen's."

"Yeah, yeah. She has magical powers that help her manipulate minds. But it doesn't always take magic." I gestured to his face, to his features that were somehow sharper, his eyes harder. "And you're different in this realm. It's screwy. Hard to tell who you are here."

He rubbed a hand over his face, eyes dark. "Yes. I know." His gaze met mine. "Let's get out of here."

He wasn't going to say more on the subject. Not now, anyway. And that was fine—because I needed to get the hell out of here and take a nap. For all my bravado and determination, I wouldn't make it back through the minefield of poison tentacles. Certainly not through the wizard's castle.

I *had* to accept his help.

"Can you transport me home?" I asked.

"Not from here. We have to go to the gate first."

"Fine." I held out a hand, grateful when his warm grip closed over me. *Close.* I was so close to getting out of here.

The ether sucked us in, spitting us out at the grand entrance to the vampire realm. The moon was bright ahead, the air cool and breezy. The white arch shined so purely in the moonlight that it looked like it was built of snow. The giant trees loomed overhead, a gorgeous set of sentries that guarded their realm.

"This place looks a hell of a lot better after where we've just been," I said.

"It does."

Felt a heck of a lot less dangerous, too. Though I wanted to gaze upon it for ages, I was more than ready to get home. "Can we get out of—"

Behind Ares, a woman appeared out of thin air. Power rolled off of her in waves, feeling like the crashing sea and smelling like the desert. Her magic felt enormous. Endless. Infinite.

I stepped to the side so that I could see her better. She was tall and blond, her slender form draped in a white catsuit that was almost futuristic.

"Who are you?" I asked.

Ares turned, then bowed. "Laima. Your high divinity."

My brows shot up. "Laima? The goddess of fate who the wizard was obsessed with?"

The catsuit was an interesting choice for an ancient goddess, but maybe she was trying to keep up with the times. If the times involved dressing like cat woman's snowy sister. *Snowball.* Wasn't that what people named white cats?

I choked back a laugh. This woman was far too impressive, and powerful, to call Snowball. Even in my head. Clearly exhaustion was getting to me.

"We must talk, Phoenix Knight." Her voice was light and airy, yet somehow still powerful.

"All right." It wasn't often that I got to talk to a god. Scratch that—it wasn't ever.

I approached. Ares stayed back, but I could feel his gaze on me. As I neared, her power signature grew stronger.

Whew. Gods were serious business, all right.

"You made quick work of Corbatt."

"Corbatt?"

"The *Burtnieki* who wouldn't take no for an answer."

"Ah, Corbatt. Yeah. Charmer, that one."

Laima grinned. "I tried to make it clear to him that no matter how *nice* he was, my interest was elsewhere. But alas. He wouldn't take no for an answer."

In fairness, Laima was super beautiful. And powerful. She was a great catch.

But not for poor Corbatt, it seemed.

"You were too busy being a goddess," I said.

"Essentially. I have duties. No time for romance. Nor interest, honestly. Particularly in his gender. Males." She shuddered.

Oh, Corbatt. Barked up the wrong tree.

"I watched you on your trials," Laima said. "I liked how you handled Corbatt, but I was particularly impressed by the volcano. Your perseverance was…stunning. You should have died."

"Thanks. I like to think of it as a poor sense of self-preservation." Where was this going?

Laima cracked a smile. "Be that as it may, I'd like to help you."

"How?" I'd take whatever help I could get, of course.

"I'm one of the three goddesses of fate here. As you are in my realm, I can peek at what is in store for you."

Fear shivered over me. "I don't think I want to know my future."

"Not your future, no. But your present."

"Present?"

"Your role in the Triumvirate has begun."

I swallowed hard. I'd expected it might have, but hadn't known for sure. Months ago, it'd been prophesied by another seer that Cass, Del, and I each had an important task to accomplish. That seer had called us the Triumvirate—three of power—though I didn't feel very powerful. Cass and Del had done their parts. *They* were powerful.

Me?

Not so much.

"So it's begun?" I shivered. "For real?"

She nodded, silver eyes gleaming in the moonlight. "Very real. It began with the Bell Beaker."

"That little clay pot from the Yorkshire Dales?"

"The very one. It's more than just a pot, as I'm sure you've guessed."

"Yeah. Some powerful people stole it, but I don't know why." My heart raced, excitement thrumming in my veins. "Do you?"

We could use any help we could get—and a goddess had to be the best kind of help.

"It is more than just a clay pot, I can tell you that. You must figure out what it is. And it is vital that you find out soon."

"Like, nowish?" In the middle of my trials for the Vampire Court? When I could hardly walk?

"Nowish."

"My friends are looking for it."

"They'll need your help. You're a vital part of this puzzle. The keystone, if I want to mix my metaphors."

"What about the people who took it? Who are they?"

Her slender shoulder shrugged. "I cannot see the fate of those not in my realm. But because you are here, I can see that you are fated to recover it—you and your friends together. But you—and only you—can stop their greater plan from coming to fruition. The world relies on you, Nix. You must succeed in your fated task for the Triumvirate."

Well that was vague. And scary. Talk about pressure. "Is there anything else you can tell me?"

"Only that you are capable. And special. And that you must persevere."

Persevere, fine. Capable, sure. Special?

That one was harder to believe. I just felt so… normal. But since I didn't know what to say, I just went with, "Oh. Okay. Thanks."

Laima smiled, as if she knew how cryptic her response had been. "Good luck, Phoenix Knight."

"Thank you."

She inclined her head. I gave an awkward little wave—how did one properly depart from a goddess?—and turned, walking back to Ares.

I was nearly to him when I stumbled, my stomach churning with that now-familiar sickness. Ares caught me by the arm, righting me.

I forced a swallow, barely controlling the urge to vomit.

"Are you all right?" he asked.

"Fine, just exhausted."

"It's more than that." Concern shadowed his gaze.

"It's nothing. Let's just get back to my place. I need a shower." The sweat and blood that coated me were beginning to itch. And the smell?

Oof.

At least Ares didn't seem to mind. He stood right next to me without even grimacing.

"Come on." I gestured. "Let's get a move on."

"Fine." *We'll finish this later.*

The subtext was clear.

But whatever—as long as he got me out of here.

I reached for his hand, grasping it tightly. He transported us away from the vampire realm. A heartbeat later, I stood on the sidewalk outside of my apartment. The cold was bracing after what I'd been through.

I stumbled, the illness making my stomach lurch. My unsettled Destroyer magic, combined with my exhaustion, was wiping me out.

Ares swept me up into his arms.

"Hey!" I wacked him on the arm, more weakly than I wanted to.

"You can barely stand. Something is obviously wrong with you." His voice was gruff. Concerned.

"I'm fine." *I wasn't fine.* "Just take me upstairs."

He nodded, stopping in front of my door. I dug my key out of my pocket and slipped it into the lock. When I withdrew it, Ares pushed the door open, then shut it behind him and climbed the stairs.

It felt too good to be in his arms as he carried me upstairs.

As soon as we entered, I shoved at him. "Put me down."

I needed distance.

He set me down. I stumbled back. "I need a shower."

I didn't wait for an acknowledgment. After the last few hours, I was just plain cranky. So I turned and headed for the tiny bathroom. Inside, I cranked on the shower water, trying not to dwell on how much I liked Ares but didn't trust him.

How could I trust him?

He was on the Vampire Court, one of the group who was forcing me into horrible trials, all while threatening to reveal my species to the Order of the Magica. Worse, it would reveal my *deirfiúr* as well.

I couldn't trust him.

But I *liked* him. And I hated that.

Was it because of the connection through his blood?

I couldn't deny that there was something there because of that. Could I trust my own feelings? I had no idea about vampire blood and what it did to a person.

Exhaustion pulled at me, distracting me from my worries.

I needed to sleep, but not like this. I was too filthy. It took all my strength to step under the hot spray of water. I propped myself against the wall, scrubbing myself clean. Thankfully, Ares's blood had closed any wounds from the tentacles. I was covered in scratches from the volcanic rock, but those only burned.

It sucked, but the pain helped keep me conscious.

Please don't let me pass out. Please, please, please.

The last thing I needed was for Ares to find me naked in the bath.

Oh fates, what if I drowned? That'd be the most embarrassing way to die ever.

Here lay Nix, drowned in the shower.

Nope. That wasn't gonna be me.

I sucked in a steadying breath and scrubbed the shampoo out of my hair, then stumbled out of the shower and wrapped a towel around my body. I was mostly dry, so I left the bathroom, peering into the living room. Ares sat on the couch.

"Be right out!" I called. I'd throw on some clothes, then ask him to leave. That'd work.

I'd made it six steps into the bedroom by the time my head started spinning. It took all I had to stagger to the bed, where I collapsed on top of the covers.

Blackness took me a moment later.

CHAPTER SEVEN

It was dark when I opened my eyes.

I jerked upright, heart pounding. Why wasn't the bathroom light on? I always left my bathroom light on. I leaned left and searched blindly for the bedside lamp.

My fingers found the base, cool and smooth, then traveled to the little knob. I twisted it, and pale yellow light filled the room.

I felt weird. Tired. Vaguely ill. My head ached like my brain had been put through a blender. What the heck had just happened?

It took a moment for my exhausted mind to click on.

Ares and I had returned from the vampire realm. He'd brought me here, where I'd promptly passed out. After showering.

I looked down, heart in my throat.

Yep. Those were my tits, out and about like they wanted a walk in the sunshine.

Damn it. Had Ares tucked me under the covers? Because I distinctly remembered passing out while wearing a towel.

A towel that was now draped over the door.

I groaned, flopping back against the headboard.

Come on. Couldn't I get a break here?

I did not need Ares seeing me naked. Perv.

My stomach grumbled, sounding like a snoring giant. After what I'd been through, no wonder I wanted a snack. The bedside clock revealed that it was 3:00 a.m.

Time for a late-night snack and some recon to see if my pervy babysitter was still in my apartment.

Since I felt too many mixed feelings about that, I focused only on dragging my sore ass out of bed and pulling on a long T-shirt and pair of raggedy shorts.

When I crept out into the dark living room, the lump on the couch confirmed my fears.

"Hey." His voice was groggy. He sat up.

I flipped on the light. It wasn't bright, but he hissed anyway. Hissed, like the freaking vampire that he was.

Too bad his tousled hair looked so damned sexy and he wasn't wearing a shirt. The *slabs of muscle* that I'd read about in romance novels were prominently on display in my living room.

The answering heat in my blood just annoyed me.

"Did you take my towel off?" I asked.

"Technically, yes. But I didn't see anything. I put you under the covers, first."

Huh. Okay. That was very gentlemanly. And decent.

Though it shouldn't be a surprise. Ares might look at me with heat in his gaze, but he also had a hell of a lot of honor. And not peeping at unconscious women ticked the honor box.

I'd have to retract my perv statement.

"Why are you here? Afraid I'm gonna run for it?" I asked.

"I wanted to make sure you were okay." He shrugged. "As for running for it—that's the whole point of letting you come home between challenges. We want you to *choose* to complete the trials and become an ally. And anyway—if you ran, I'd find you."

Ugh. Didn't I know it. "I'm going to get something to eat. You hungry?"

"Yeah." He stood, scrubbing a hand through his hair as if to flatten it. It didn't work. But I liked the result anyway.

I turned away, heading toward the kitchen. As I neared it, I realized that Ares looked different. Back to his normal, earthly self. No more blade-sharp cheekbones and cold eyes.

Since I couldn't handle the bright light in the kitchen, I ignored the switch and went straight to the fridge. I grabbed two sports drinks and a big bowl of leftover macaroni and cheese from the other day.

It only took a few minutes to heat in the microwave, then I divided it into two bowls and carried my loot out to the living room. It was awkward, with the sports drinks tucked under my arms and the bowls in my hands, but I managed.

Ares stood at the window, peering out at the night as if looking for predators.

"See anything good?" I asked as I clumsily set the bowls on the table. The bottles dropped out from under my arms and plopped on the rug. I fished them out from under the coffee table, then sat.

"No. Quiet night." He turned to face me.

"I'd say that's good."

"Given your situation, I'd agree." He joined me on the couch, sitting on the far end.

"So my situation is that bad, huh?"

"You're getting ill frequently, so I'd say yes."

Shit. I thought he'd meant my situation with the Vampire Court. But no. He was cleverer than that. And he was fishing.

I pointed to the bowl of mac and cheese closest to him. "That's yours."

"Thanks." He picked it up and began eating.

I followed suit, chowing down. As long as I was chewing, I wasn't answering questions. And I was famished, anyway.

I barely came up for air. By the time the bowl was empty, I felt a lot better. The red sports drink was cool and quenching, tasting like sweet chemicals. Delightful. Only then did I realize how dehydrated I'd been. No wonder I had a headache.

I wanted to get up and get a painkiller, but I was just too damned tired. So I slumped back against the couch. Every inch of my body felt like it'd been poured onto the sofa.

"There's a lot you're not telling me, Nix."

I tilted my head on the cushion, gazing at him through tired eyes. "Back at you, champ."

But he didn't look like a champ—not like the little kid version or even the MVP ballplayer kind. He looked big and strong and dangerous. And he was here in my living room, with all kinds of power over me and my future.

It made me antsy.

"Why do you get ill?" he asked. "Just randomly, you'll stumble and look like you're going to be sick."

I shrugged. "I eat crap I shouldn't."

"Don't hide things from me, Nix." He turned to me, gaze intent. "I can help you. I want to help you."

Thing was, I kinda believed him. He still made me nervous, and I had no idea what his true end goal was, but he seemed sincere about trying to help me. I couldn't trust that he wouldn't do things I despised—like kidnapping the Kevins of the world—but he'd made it clear he wanted to help me as much as he could.

"There's stuff I don't know about you, too," I said. "Kinda scary stuff."

"We'll trade," he said.

"Like, you show me yours and I show you mine?"

"Basically." His voice roughened. "I'm always interested in seeing yours."

I scowled, but only to hide the flush. Because I could feel his attraction to me. Not in the normal way, either. But deeper. Like there was something connecting us.

"You said there'd be no side effects of sharing your blood," I said. "But I feel a connection to you. A weird one."

His brow furrowed. "That's not normal."

"Well, it's there. I thought I felt it after you healed me in London. But now I definitely do."

He propped his strong arms on his knees, staring at his steepled hands. It looked like he was really trying to figure this out. And coming up short.

"You really have no idea." And that scared me.

He turned, his gaze hot on me. "I know that you're special, Nix. You can walk in the Shadowlands. Now you're telling me that my blood has given you some kind of connection to me."

Shit. I'd thought I was accusing him of withholding some kind of secret vampire mojo from me.

What if I'd been revealing more of my mysterious weirdness?

Not good.

"Why do you look so scary in the vampire realm? And your eyes are colder." The words spilled from my lips. I wanted to know, but I also wanted to distract him from dwelling on my weirdness.

Of course it didn't work.

"You've already had your question," he said. "Now you have to show me yours."

"Then you get two questions in a row. Just answer this one."

He nodded. "Fine. That place brings out the vampiric nature. I become...*more*... there."

"And that's why you prefer it in the human realm."

His mouth kicked up at the corner. "I see what you did there. You phrased it as a statement, but it's actually a question."

I shrugged.

"Fine," he said. "But you'll owe me. You're right, though. I prefer earth. Unlike the rest of the vampires in the realm, I have a halfbreed side. That side makes me prefer earth. My humanity is smothered in the vampire realm, and I don't like it."

"I kinda noticed that." I preferred this Ares. The more human one.

"Does your sickness have to do with the fact that you stole powers from Aleric, the man who killed Marin?" Ares asked.

Shock raced through me, chilling my skin. I hadn't told Ares I'd done that. As usual, I'd only told my *deirfiúr*. And I'd made sure that no one saw me take those powers.

"Don't try to deny it, Nix. It's obvious what happened. He fell and sustained a mortal wound. Taking his power was the only smart thing to do."

"Smart?"

"Yes. You're smart. And I'm not an idiot."

I rolled my neck so that I stared at the ceiling. "Fine. I took his Destroyer power. But I haven't had time to practice controlling it, so it makes me ill."

"Then you need to practice."

"I know that."

"*Soon.* As in, tomorrow. Or now. With the sickness hitting you at unknown times, you may not survive the next challenge."

I swallowed hard. "I know. I *know.* Tomorrow I will."

"Good. Now, what's the Triumvirate?"

My head whipped toward him. Or tried to. The exhaustion was creeping back on me, despite the importance of his question.

"I heard Laima mention the Triumvirate, and that you're part of it. And that you have a great task to accomplish."

"Eavesdrop much?"

"It's how I get the best information. So what is it?"

I yawned, exhaustion tugging at me. My eyelids weighed a thousand pounds. "Haven't we talked enough?"

"Are you trying to avoid the question or are you tired?"

I shrugged, my eyelids finally losing the battle. "Why not both?"

Ares chuckled low.

It was the last thing I heard.

~

The second time I woke, my face was pressed into one of my couch pillows. Groggily, I scrubbed a hand over my eyes and sat up.

Dawn sunlight cut through the blinds, striping across the rug. My eyes flared wide.

What time was it?

Laima's warning about the beaker flashed in my mind. Now that I was recovered and well-rested, my responsibilities were battering their way into my mind.

If Ares were still in my apartment, he wasn't in the living room with me. He must have stretched me out on the couch last night after I'd fallen asleep as a defense mechanism—like a fainting goat.

I dragged myself off the couch, then hurried into the kitchen, shutting the door and leaning against it. I pressed my fingertips to the comms charm around my neck.

"Cass? Del?"

"Hey!" Cass's voice sounded bright and chipper.

"How are you?" Del asked.

"Pass the vamp test with flying colors?" Cass added.

"I passed, at least. Have you discovered anything about the beaker?"

"Yeah, a bit," Cass said. "Want to meet in an hour at P&P? Go over some things?"

I glanced at the clock over the stove. 8 a.m. right now. "Yeah. Nine would be perfect."

"Great, see you then," Cass said.

"Later!" Del added.

I cut the connection with the comms charm and grabbed an energy drink out of the fridge, chugging the first half of the sweet stuff.

The apartment was quiet as I crept through the living room toward the bathroom and bedroom. I held my breath as I peered into the bedroom.

Ares was sprawled over my bed, shirt off and hair tousled.

Gulp.

He looked too damned good. And this was too damned intimate. Seeing him in my bed made warmth flush through me. Warmth that I definitely wasn't prepared to think about.

"Hey!" I shouted.

Ares popped up, eyes alert.

"Comfy?" I asked.

"Very." His voice was sleep roughened. "You look better. Feel all right?"

"One hundred percent. But you need to scram." I hiked a thumb toward the living room. "I need to change and meet my friends in an hour."

Ares glanced at the bedside clock. "You can use that hour to practice your magic. You're going to need it."

It wasn't a bad idea. But what did he mean by *I was going to need it?* "Do you know something about my next task?"

He nodded. "Starts this afternoon."

"No break. Of course."

"What do you call last night?"

"Fair point." But considering that I had to help my *deirfiúr* track down an invaluable archaeological and magical treasure, I needed more time. But since I wasn't going to get it, I'd have to make do with what I had. I waved for him to get up. "Come on, get."

He climbed out of bed, wearing just his boxer briefs. I spun around eyeing the window and trying to banish the image of muscular thighs. "You can change in the living room."

The problem with my suggestion was that it meant he walked in front of me in just his tight black underwear.

The butt on that dude...

I squeezed my eyes shut and turned to my bedroom. It didn't take long to rifle through my clothes—thank fates I'd done the laundry before this madness started. I pulled out a kitty Princess

Leia shirt and tugged it on, completing it with my usual jeans and motorcycle boots. A leather jacket finished the ensemble.

As I returned to the living room, I took stock of my magic. The rest and recover had done wonders, refilling me nearly to the brim.

Ares waited for me in the living room, completely dressed, thankfully.

"Why are you still here?" I asked.

"You looked like hell last night. I thought you could use the help."

"Thanks. But why are you here *now?*" I was healthy now. I didn't need to be back to the Vampire Court until this afternoon.

"I like you, Nix. And I figured I could give you a ride to some-place where you can practice your magic without causing problems."

Huh. The way he said it... so out in the open. No shifty games or hinting. And he did have a point. My new magic was destruc-tion. I needed to go somewhere where I wouldn't destroying things I shouldn't.

"Thanks," I said. "Any idea where we should go? It needs to be somewhere empty. No people or valuable things that I could hurt."

He smiled, as if glad I'd agreed to go with him. "I have an idea. But you'll have to bring some things to practice on."

"Not a problem." I hurried to the kitchen, grabbing an iron pot that had a broken handle. I'd hated to throw it away, but it was in such bad shape I couldn't really use it.

Now, it'd help me practice my magic. Not a bad way to go.

Then I grabbed a burned dishrag and a pencil that had been sharpened down to a nub. None of it was as big as the stuff I'd seen Aleric destroy with this gift, but you had to start somewhere.

I carried my loot back to the living room. "Ready to go!"

Ares turned to face me. The sun cut across his face, caressing his features. For a creature of the night, he sure looked good in the sun. He held out a hand.

I took it, trying not to focus on how strong he felt.

"Hang on," he said.

I grinned. A moment later, the ether sucked us in.

When I opened my eyes on the other side, I gasped.

The land stretched out flat and white in front of us, gleaming under the light of the full moon. The moonlight reflected so brightly that it was easy to see. The sight was eerily beautiful, the night silent and warm.

"Where are we?" I breathed. "This place is incredible."

"It's the Rann of Kutch, in Rajasthan, India. One of the largest salt deserts in the world."

"Wow." I spun in a circle, taking in the beautiful emptiness around me. There wasn't much here—just the flat white ground that must be covered in salt and the full moon—but the place was magnificent in its simplicity.

"Perfect place, right?"

"Yeah. Really is." I sat on the white ground and spread my loot out before me. The salt was grainy beneath me, making me wish for a giant Margarita despite the early hour. Though, technically, it was about eight at night here. So, after happy hour. I grinned, then banished the thought to focus on the task at hand. "I'm going to get started."

Except, I had no idea what to do. I'd tried practicing this magic the day before yesterday, but had had no luck. Both my *deirfiúr* had tried to help, giving me their techniques for learning a new skill, but it hadn't worked.

It'd been a long time since I'd had to practice my conjuring.

"You're lost," Ares said.

I looked up at him, standing tall in the moonlight.

"Kinda," I said. "It's just that it's so contrary to my normal magic. I'm used to creating. Destroying is so...weird."

And wrong. I knew destruction *could* be a good thing. But in so many cases, it wasn't. Especially not the way I'd seen Aleric use this gift. He'd blown apart metal stairs and nearly destroyed a great metal door.

Those could be handy skills to have. And even if I didn't get that level of control, I at least had to come to peace with the new magic within me so that I didn't keep getting sick.

"What have you tried before?" Ares asked.

"Um, visualization. My friend Del imagines her magic as a light that she controls. But it didn't work for me."

"No, I can see how that might not work for everyone." Ares looked thoughtful. "But visualization is a good technique. It worked for me while I was learning my powers as a child."

"You have a lot, don't you?"

"From my mother, yes. She was very talented."

So far I'd seen his gift for creating light and walking through foreign realms. Not to mention the healing power in his blood. I wondered what else he had up his sleeve.

The breeze blew across my face, feeling divine. It sparked an idea. "I could try something else, maybe. Give me a moment."

I hadn't had a lot of time to practice before. We'd been too busy dealing with the aftermath of Aleric and returning the beaker to its proper resting place—where it no longer was.

But now I had time. And I had to come up with something good.

The cool breeze brushed past my cheek again. It was so lovely, giving me energy and strength.

An idea popped into my head. Wind.

It could build things—like sand dunes—or it could destroy. Every hurricane and tornado was proof of that. Maybe I shouldn't have envisioned my magic as light like Del did. Wind made more sense.

I closed my eyes and drew in a deep breath. It was easy to feel the Destroyer's magic in my body. It felt like sickness. A vague nausea that stayed with me always, roaring up to attack at inopportune moments.

The wind rustled across my hair and I focused on it, drawing it within myself. I could *feel* it. I'd have bet twenty bucks this wasn't visualization at all. Wind roared through me, circling around inside my chest, drawing up the sickness into a small ball.

With a trembling hand, I reached out and touched the pencil stub, then forced the wind through my arm and into the slender bit of wood.

The Destroyer magic followed the wind. I peeked, watching. Hoping.

The pencil looked the same.

I sucked in a deep breath and forced more wind into it, praying the destruction magic followed along.

The pencil began to crack, splintering down the middle.

"You're doing it," Ares said. "Keep going."

I did, feeding the pencil more and more of the destroying wind. At this point, I was creating the wind as much as I was absorbing it from the atmosphere.

Finally, the pencil shattered into dust.

I collapsed, barely supporting myself on my hands. Suddenly, I realize how much the magic had taken out of me. Sweat cooled on my brow and my muscles ached.

"Wow, that's hard," I gasped.

Ares crouched down and met my gaze. "You did great."

His voice was...proud, almost. But not patronizing. I had a good ear for that. Suddenly, I realized how close he was. His hand was on the ground near my knee and he was only a foot from me.

At this distance, I could smell his intoxicating scent. The winter morning smell of his magic, combined with something that was distinctly him. Clean and earthy at the same time.

Up close, he was so handsome it made my breath catch in my throat.

I shouldn't be this affected by him, but I was. He wove a spell around me, some kind of vampire mojo—except that existed only in the movies.

This was all Ares.

His gaze dropped to my lips, his green eyes darkening with heat. I felt it too, as if he were a sexual space heater.

I couldn't help it—my gaze dropped to his lips as well. I swallowed hard, licking my lower lip. Ares leaned in, just slightly.

My mind filled with visions of kissing his full lips. Of pushing him onto his back and climbing on top of him.

The closeness—and the visions—snapped some sense into me.

Now was *not* the time. I had to practice my magic. I had to meet with my *deirfiúr* and solve this mystery. And I had to learn to trust Ares.

He was a guy with too many sides—the harsh vampire who put me through my trials in the vampire realm and the more human one who was helping me.

Who was he? Because there was only one I should trust, and I didn't know which one he really was.

"Um, I need to practice some more," I said.

His gaze cleared immediately, as if he realized my sudden discomfort. He leaned back. "Yes. Practice. It's vital."

"Yeah." I inspected the dust that used to be the pencil. The dishrag sat next to it, looking impossibly big. "I have a long way to go."

Ares stood, moving off to the side. "You'll get there."

He was right—I would. I would have to.

It took a while, but I managed to destroy the dishtowel. I was exhausted by the time I was done, and since I still had to face another Vampire Court challenge, I didn't want to waste any more magic or energy.

What I really needed was breakfast.

Ares transported us to P&P in a flash. It was cold and rainy, the wind whipping across my cheeks. I shivered and stepped away, my broken cooking pot tucked under my arm.

Cass popped out of P&P a moment later, apparently having seen us appear.

She pointed to the pot. "What's that?"

"My badge of shame. I couldn't destroy it."

"But she destroyed a pencil and a dishtowel," Ares said.

"Well done!" Cass clapped me on the back. "But you've got a ways to go."

I grinned. "At least I can count on you for your honesty."

"Always. Come on. Let's have some breakfast and chat."

I glanced at Ares. We hadn't yet told him our suspicions about the dragon tattoo gang who'd been responsible for Marin's death. No doubt he was interested—probably even doing research of his own.

But I didn't want to talk about that yet. First, I'd find out what Cass and Del had discovered. Then, I'd weasel what information I could out of Ares.

"So, I was thinking that we could meet back up after I have breakfast with my friends?" *Please be cool with it.*

He nodded. "I'd like a change of clothes, and I have a meeting with Magisteria and Doyen. I'll meet you back here in three hours to pick you up for your next trial."

Cass's eyes widened. "Another one? Today? But you just finished one."

"I know." And I was still kind of feeling it. Well rested, but with sore muscles. Practicing my magic this morning hadn't helped. But since Ares had insisted, I had to think it would help me with my upcoming trial.

Ares nodded at Cass, then turned his gaze to me. "I'll see you soon."

"Bye." I waved awkwardly, and he disappeared.

Cass turned to me, gaze relieved. "Thank fates he's gone."

"Yeah. Yeah, totally."

Cass poked me in the shoulder, her brows raised. "Oh my gosh. You aren't glad he's gone at all. You *do* like him."

"No. Totally not. Well, I mean, kinda. But I can't trust him, so it doesn't matter."

"Why not?"

"He's on the Vampire Court. Putting me through crazy trials that exploit my weakness. Which I think he may be telling Magisteria and Doyen all about." Right now, in fact. He could be telling them about my Destroyer gift and the problems I was having.

But he'd also healed me.

So yeah, who the hell knew?

"Let's not worry about him now," I said. "Let's talk about what you learned, and then I'll see if I can get any info out of him."

Cass nodded. "Good plan."

I followed her into P&P. It was warm and cozy, with that cotton-wool feeling of being protected from a stormy winter morning. Quiet music played on the speakers, something that Connor had picked out for a rainy day. He had perfect taste.

Since it was a weekday, the morning crowd had died down. There were old guys doing the crossword puzzle in the corner, but otherwise, it was just me and my friends. Connor stood behind the counter, his dark hair flopped over his head, fiddling with the controls of the huge, gleaming espresso machine.

Del waved from our usual spot at the comfy chairs in the corner. I joined her, sinking gratefully into the plush softness of my usual chair. I'd need a cat nap before meeting Ares again, just to recoup some of my power.

Claire hurried over, her brown hair pulled back into a ponytail and an apron over her fighting leathers. She smiled. "The usual?"

"Yeah, thanks." I grinned at her. "You're a hero."

She winked, then hurried back to the counter.

I turned back to Cass and Del. "So, you found something?"

Cass pushed her red hair back from her face and leaned forward. "We tracked them. Del and I went back to the caves on the Yorkshire Dales first. Just to see if they'd left anything behind that would help our dragon senses latch onto them."

"And? How was the site? Much destruction?"

"Fortunately, only a few of the artifacts were destroyed. The rockfall was mostly contained to one side."

"Whew. Good." My muscles relaxed a bit. I'd been worried about that.

Claire returned with our food—their special breakfast pasties and coffee—then sat down to join us. She often helped us out when we had problems like this. Right now, we could use all the help we could get.

She looked at Cass and Del. "You're telling Nix about what you found?"

"Yeah." Del lowered her voice. "We found a boot under the rocks. Foot still in it."

I slowed the pastry that I was putting to my mouth. "Ew."

"Yeah." Del grimaced. "That mage who caused the rockfall didn't have as much control as he thought he did, I guess. Anyway, that definitely gave us enough to find the guys who did this. They live—or work—in a huge warehouse compound on the northwest side of town. In the woods."

Del handed me her cell phone. I took it, studying the photo. Though the huge trees, an enormous factory building rose up from cleared grounds. Guards were stationed on the porch and all around the perimeter. Dozens of them.

"That's a lot of guards. And that place is on the outskirts of Magic's Bend?" I looked up, flabbergasted.

"Yeah," Cass said. "Kinda crazy. That factory building is old, but the fences and security are new."

I turned back to the phone, flipping through. There was a

massive gate, more guards, some guard-dogs that I could see. And in one, the ocean. "It overlooks the sea."

"Yes," Del said. "On one side are the gates and dogs and magical enchantments that give Aidan's a run for their money. On the other side is the sea."

"So you weren't able to get in?"

"We didn't try very hard," Cass said. "It was clear we'd need more backup. And Aidan is checking to see if his company has something that can counter their magical protections."

It wouldn't be the first time we used Aidan's skills in security to break through magical barriers.

"And none of us even knew about this place?" I certainly hadn't. But then I kept to this part of Magic's Bend, for the most part. We all did.

"No. It's well hidden, and pretty far off the beaten path. And I can't imagine they've been there super long." Cass leaned forward, eyes intense. "But here's the crazy thing. We saw the guards. And two of them had visible tattoos of dragons."

Excitement and dread competed within me. "Holy fates. So then the fragment of tattoo we saw on the mage had to be a dragon. And the dragon gang is involved in the theft of the beaker."

I leaned back, mind spinning.

"If they're even a gang," Del said. "I don't know a lot about gangs, but that compound we saw was high budget, despite the old factory they've got it in. And professional."

"So more like a mob?" I asked. What exactly was the difference?

"Or some other terrifying organization." Cass held up her fingers and began to tick off. "So far, they've murdered an Informa mage—Marin Olerafort—to steal his secret about drag-ons. They abducted you with the intent to kill or torture you for information, and they've stolen this beaker. Oh, and they defi-nitely wouldn't have minded killing us during those attacks."

"No, they wouldn't." They'd tried with the giant spiders and the rockfalls. Those weren't subtle attempts. "So some serious shit is happening."

"Yeah." Del shoved her dark hair back from her face, blue eyes annoyed. "They're planning something, obviously. We can't ignore the secret that they killed Marin for."

"Dragons. Returned." It'd been only two words, pulled from the mind of Marin's killer, along with a string of others that had been unintelligible. The prophecy had been protected—scrambled, more like—by the Cathar Perfecti who had held onto the secret for centuries.

Though I'd taken the secret from Aleric by stealing his Informa ability, I hadn't been able to decipher it myself.

"And you still don't know if Aleric told his mysterious master the information he'd stolen from Marin?" Claire asked.

"We don't." I scrubbed a weary hand over my face and sipped the coffee she'd brought. "But I think it's safe to assume he did."

"And somehow the beaker is connected," Del said.

"Or at least valuable and part of some other plan," Cass added.

Del leaned back in her chair, staring at the ceiling. "Which we can assume is evil, given the magic that came off that compound."

"Gross?" I asked. Normally, evil magic and intentions gave off disgusting signature. Garbage fire scents, jellyfish stings, the screeching of nails on chalkboard. That sort of thing.

"Totally gross." Del straightened, her face set in a grimace. "Totally evil."

"Perfect." I bit into a cheese and potato pasty, forcing myself to take in some energy. I'd need it, that was for sure. I swallowed and looked at my three friends. "I met a goddess of fate in the vampire realm."

Three pairs of eyebrows shot upward.

"A real goddess?" Claire asked.

"Totally real. You should have felt her magic." Just the memory of its strength sent shivers across my skin. "She was the

105

real deal. Anyway, she told me that my role in the Triumvirate has begun."

"Geez, this is all happening fast," Cass said. "All in the space of a year. Me, Del, then you."

"Maybe we'll get it out of the way," Del said.

"Or die." We'd barely survived the last two challenges presented to us by fate.

"Not die," Claire said. "You can handle this. And we'll help, of course."

I reached over and squeezed her hand. "Thanks. I bet we'll need it."

Though Claire made a mean pasty and could sling drinks with the best of them, her real skill was with a sword and her fire mage skills. If she turned her mercenary abilities toward our problems, we'd have a better chance, without question.

"What else did the goddess say?" Del asked.

"That the beaker is more than a beaker. And it's important to my task for the Triumvirate."

"So this just jumped up a priority level, huh?" Cass asked.

"Definitely." I polished off the last of the pasty. "I have another Vampire Court trial to complete in a couple hours. If I can win their trust, they'll be off our backs. And maybe even help us."

"That's worth striving for," Del said. "We'll do another round of recon, this time with Aidan and his tools. Scout for weaknesses so we can break in later."

"I like it." I looked hard at them. "But don't go in without me."

"Wouldn't dream of it," Cass said.

"Better not," I said. Whatever this was, it was dangerous. I knew my *deirfiúr* were strong—stronger than me, in fact—but the idea of them going off to fix this alone made me nervous. It was my task. My danger to face. I didn't want them at risk for something I should be doing.

I couldn't lose them.

CHAPTER EIGHT

I managed to snag two hours of sleep on my couch before Ares showed up outside my apartment. Once again, he did the tossing pebbles at the window thing. The clattering against the glass woke me.

I scrambled up, wiping a bit of drool from my face, then hurried to the window. I pushed it open to see him standing out in the light rain, his hair sparkling with it.

"You really need to give me your phone number," he called up.

"I rarely have it turned on." With my comms charm, I didn't often need it. "I'll come get you."

Since we didn't have any kind of fancy buzzer on the green door at the foot of the stairs, I ran down to open the door. He grinned and stepped in.

"What are you looking so cheery about?" I was grumpy, having been woken up to go get my butt kicked in the vampire realm.

"Just glad to see you."

That was too honest. And too nice. Instead of responding—since I didn't know how to respond to such a normal sentiment in such un-normal times—I turned and hurried back upstairs.

Ares followed, though I had to glance back to confirm that since his steps were so silent.

"You ready to go?" he asked.

"Just about." I tugged on my boot, then pulled on a leather jacket over top of my kitty Princess Leia shirt. I hurried into the kitchen, whipping up a quick cheese sandwich. Just cheese on bread, really, since I didn't have time for the fixings. But I'd need all the energy I could get for what was coming.

I returned to the living room, swallowing the first bite of my sandwich. "So, the challenge will start right away?"

Ares nodded and held out a hand.

I walked to him and took it. When the ether sucked us in, I barely noticed. I was getting used to this. I'd transported plenty of times before, but it was becoming so commonplace with Ares that it was like stepping out the door.

When we arrived in the vampire realm, it looked the same as it had. Big full moon shining down on the white marble gate and the massive, silver-leafed trees standing guard.

"Does this place always look the same?" I asked.

"Essentially. It rains sometimes. But there are two moons, so something is always up in the sky."

"Two moons? So this place is somewhere else in the solar system?"

"Honestly, we don't know how it works." Ares started toward the gate.

I followed, eating my sandwich as I walked.

"We have vampire scholars, of course," Ares said. "But none have figured out the two-moon thing. We know how to access our realm from earth, and that it shares cultural similarities with the Baltic. But otherwise, we don't know."

This place was full of mysteries. The walk down the path bordered by statues was as riveting as it had been the first time. Honestly, despite the challenges I faced here, I liked the vampire realm. It was magical in the purest sense of the word.

I glanced at Ares as we walked, noting that his features had taken on the sharp harshness of the vampire realm. He was almost more handsome, but in a way that made fearful chills race over me.

As we neared the courtyard where Doyen and Magisteria spent much of their time, nerves began to prickle my skin. It was hard to swallow the last bite of sandwich, but I valiantly managed.

Once again, Doyen and Magisteria sat in their thrones. When they looked up, they were even scarier than Ares. Their features were sharper, their gazes colder.

"You are ready?" Doyen asked.

I shivered at the sound of her voice, remembering the mind games she'd played with me. And with poor Kevin. Before I'd taken my nap earlier, I'd tracked him down and given him a call to make sure he was all right. Fortunately, he was.

I looked at Doyen. "Ready as I'll ever be."

She stood, Magisteria along with her, and tucked a hand inside her white robe, withdrawing a piece of parchment. She held it out, her gaze expectant. I approached, heart pounding, and took the paper.

It was thick and sturdy. I unfolded it. "A map?"

"Yes. You must reach the X at the other end," Magisteria.

"What's there?" On the paper, it was literally just an X. There were written directions scrawled on the map, which showed a land I'd never seen before. The vampire realm, presumably.

"You'll find out," Doyen said.

"Ares will accompany you." Annoyance coated Magisteria's voice.

"Again?" I asked.

"Again." Ares's voice was hard, his gaze on Magisteria and Doyen.

Magisteria scowled at him. "Normally, one of us would take the second challenge. But he has insisted."

Though they were a trio—each equal in power, supposedly—it was obvious that they didn't want to fight him on this. Point to Ares in the vampire power struggle.

Doyen gestured to the sea beyond, which shined silver in the moonlight. "You may begin."

I nodded to them, the best I could do in terms of a polite goodbye, and looked down at the map. As she'd indicated, it directed me toward the sea. So I turned and walked toward it.

The body of water was massive. I couldn't see all the way across, and it disappeared along the horizon to both the left and the right. The waves were tiny, lapping at the black sand shore. What lurked beneath the depths?

I shuddered at the thought.

A small rowboat was beached just out of reach of the waves, its worn gray wood looking like it'd seen better days. I glanced at the map.

As I'd feared, the map said to board the boat. Since I saw no engine, I had a feeling this wasn't going to be an easy trip.

Ares approached to stand next to me and glanced down. "Ready?"

"Yep." I walked toward the boat, catching sight of the oars within. Before pushing the thing out onto the sea, I crouched at the water and dipped my fingers in, then raised them to my lips.

Freshwater. Thank fates for small favors.

I turned to Ares. "Give me a hand with the boat? Or is that against the rules?"

"Small things are fine."

Together, we pushed the boat out onto the water. I hopped in, narrowly avoiding getting my boots wet, and Ares followed.

I bent down and grabbed done of the heavy oars, then stood at one end of the boat—I had no idea if it was the bow or the stern—and stuck the oar into the water, pushing us off of the beach.

We drifted out onto the gleaming silver sea, the moon

sparkling down upon us. Ares stood at the end of the boat, watching to see what I would do. It really felt like a test.

I unfolded the map and studied it. We needed to go directly across, which the map said was precisely due west. I glanced around, searching for a compass. Nothing.

So I conjured one, the task fortunately taking only a small amount of power since the compass was small and I was well practiced at conjuring them. They often came in handy.

I picked up the other oar. "I suppose I'm starting?"

"If you like. Though I can help with that, too."

"I'll start." I sat and locked the oars into the little wooden bits that held them, and began to row. It was awkward at first, but I got the hang of it.

Ares sat at the bow of the boat, behind me, so I didn't have to be distracted by his too-handsome, and slightly scary, face. But I swore I could feel his gaze on me like a brand. It seared my skin.

The little boat cut across the surface of the silver sea, the oars swishing through the water. So that I would row in the right direction, I kept my eye on two landmarks on the shore—a huge white palace on a hill and a tree that was larger than all the rest, spearing into the sky until it looked like it touched the moon.

I got into a rhythm with the oars, carrying us far enough out that I lost track of the shore. Without my landmarks, I had to consult the compass to keep heading west, but fortunately I hadn't deviated too far off.

"Any clues where we're going?" I asked Ares.

"Unfortunately, no."

"So you don't know, or you won't say?"

"Don't know. I had a hand in designing the challenge, but most of the details are a mystery."

"Hhmmpfh." I pulled hard on the oars, determined to get across in record time. The moon sparkled on the silver sea. There were even a few stars in the sky, glittering down.

Out here, it was quiet save for the oars cutting through the water and the waves lapping at the hull of the boat. A cool breeze brushed the hair off my face as I rowed.

It was starting to feel truly zen when the boat vibrated.

I shot out of my rowing trance, gaze darting around. The hull of the boat continued to vibrate. Bubbles popped to the surface all around us. They were bursting against the bottom of the boat.

"Ah, hell," Ares muttered.

"What do you—"

A massive tentacle shot out of the sea to our left. It was at least twenty feet long and as big around as a horse. It shimmered jade green, glinting in the moonlight.

There was no land in sight and a giant squid was right below us.

"What is it?" I demanded as I pulled harder on the oars, trying to force us away from the monster.

"Kraken."

Another tentacle burst out of the water to the right, splashing me with cool water. I yanked on the oars, but was too slow. The tentacle wrapped around our boat, right in front of me.

I jerked the oars in, tossing them into the hull, and scrambled back toward Ares as the Kraken began to lift the little boat out of the sea.

It was a huge beast, and had at least six more arms where these had come from. As tempted as I was to conjure a sword and chop off a limb, it was a terrible idea.

"We can't fight it." My mind raced. It was too big, too strong, and totally in its element.

"Nope."

And Ares wouldn't transport us out of here. I tumbled against Ares as the Kraken raised us five feet above the water. My heart thundered in my chest as its head broke the surface. It was huge, a glinting jade green with eyes like gleaming emeralds.

The Kraken opened its mouth wide, pink flesh gleaming

inside. He was going to tip us right into his mouth. My heartbeat thundered, defeating inside my head.

We were dinner.

The Kraken had another idea, though. A third tentacle rose out of the sea and plucked me out of the boat, wrapping around my waist and hoisting me into the air. Upside down.

My stomach heaved as the Kraken waved me around, its tentacle tight around me. Squeezing, squeezing, squeezing.

Ares shouted. I caught sight of him, rage and fear on his face.

My head swam and my heart raced. The Kraken dangled me right over his mouth. A scream strangled in my throat as my skin chilled at the thought of being eaten. Swallowed alive. But the thought popped an idea into my head.

He's hungry.

And since he wanted to eat *us*, I'd bet he wasn't a vegetarian.

Quickly, I conjured a huge tuna steak and dropped it into his mouth. His jaw clamped down on it. A weird purring sound of delight followed.

Please don't eat me, now.

"Good thinking," Ares shouted. "More!"

I was already on it, conjuring as quickly as I could. As soon as the giant squid opened his mouth again, I dropped another tuna steak into the gaping maw.

Chomp.

Purr.

It made a wet smacking sound. I'd used this trick before, but never on a Kraken.

Sweat beaded on my skin as I watched the giant monster swallow. How much could he eat? Could I even conjure enough?

I'd sure as hell have to try, since the alternative was him dropping me into his craw.

Blood rushed in my head as I conjured and tossed. I felt like an animal trainer at a sea park, feeding the hungry beast as the crowd roared. Except, the roaring was coming from inside my head as I tried to keep my cool.

Eventually, the Kraken closed its maw for good, eyeing me with its glittery green eyes.

"Tasty?" My words were strangled. Most of my blood had to be in my head by now.

It didn't answer me, but since it also didn't open its mouth again, I claimed a small victory. When it set me back down in the boat, I collapsed, gasping and clinging to the railing. Slowly, the Kraken lowered the boat back onto the water. It splashed down.

My breath held as I watched the glittery green monster sink beneath the surface of the sea.

"Holy crap," I gasped.

Ares helped me up. My ribs ached and my shirt was wet from the Kraken's grip, but a slow deep breath revealed that there were no cracked ribs.

"That was nuts." I'd just fought the Kraken. Or fed the Kraken. Whatever. "You vampires sure love your squids."

Ares grinned. "Coincidence."

"Sure." I plopped back down on the middle bench, catching my breath. When I felt a bit more human, I picked up my oars and popped them back into place.

"Why don't I take over?" Ares said.

I glanced up at him. "Sure thing. Not gonna look a gift horse in the mouth."

I scrambled back to the seat in the bow and let him take my place. My muscles ached from rowing and I could use the break.

"Where are the Pūķi?" I asked. "Those little dragons were so helpful last time."

"They can't fly over water."

My eyes sharpened. "Is that why the challenge takes place over water? So they can't help me out?"

"One of the reasons, yes."

"Jerks."

As he picked up the oars, I consulted my compass again. "Get the bow pointing slightly more to the left. Your left."

He pulled on the right oar, spinning us.

"Good!"

Ares began to row. I couldn't help but admire the play of his muscles beneath his shirt, or the speed with which we cut through the water. I dragged my gaze away, studying our surroundings.

Water as far as the eye could see. Not a speck of land. And more dangers, all hidden beneath the silvery surface.

Ares rowed for what felt like hours. I kept up my guard, inspecting the water all around, and kept track with the compass. When the water started to glitter, I almost didn't notice. It looked so much like the silvery sheen that was already there.

Except that it was definitely different. Sparkling and shining. Tiny electric blue lights, the size of pinheads.

It was gorgeous.

When the first little monster leapt out of the sea, I shrieked. It splatted onto the arm of my leather jacket arm. Instinctually, I brushed it off.

Electric pain blazed through my hand. *"Shit!"*

"Don't touch them!" Ares said. "Electric jellyfish. Too many stings and you're dead."

All around the boat, tiny jellyfish floated to the surface, glittery and gleaming. Some popped out of the water, leaping for us.

Another landed on my neck, sending a shock through my whole body. I convulsed briefly, stopping only when the jellyfish fell of and plopped into the bottom of the boat.

Ares pulled hard on the oars, trying to get us away from our tiny attackers. But size did not directly correlate to deadliness. Even ants could kill you, if there were enough of them.

And there were enough jellyfish. They set the surface of the water alight with their electric sparkles. No matter how fast Ares rowed, they surrounded our boat, occasionally flying out to land on us.

My skin chilled with fear. I was about to conjure rain suits—anything to keep us from being hit—when a giant boulder appeared at the other end of the boat.

The weight of the boulder pressed that side of the boat lower into the water, throwing me against Ares's back.

"What the hell!" I scrambled back. Ares followed, redistributing the weight more evenly.

We almost sank right then and there, but our quick thinking kept the stern of the boat from dipping below the surface of the water.

"What the hell, Ares? A boulder in a boat?" It had to weigh hundreds of pounds.

"That's not all." He pointed to the base of the boulder.

I glanced down, seeing metal spikes protruding from the bottom of the rock. They pierced the boat's hull. Water was seeping in, slowly but surely. And it wouldn't take much to fill a tiny boat like this.

Then we'd sink and be electrocuted to death by tiny jellyfish. Water was already lapping around my boots. Jellyfish floated in it, glittering and deadly.

Shit, shit, shit.

"I'm going to conjure another boat," I said.

"Another rock will appear," Ares said.

"I thought you didn't know what was going to happen." The water was to my ankles now. My heart pounded.

"I don't. But it's only logical. You've already conjured something to save us. Now use your other skills."

My gaze darted to him. "My other skills?"

His dark gaze met mine, serious. "Your other skills. The ones you've practiced."

"Oh, shit." I'd only managed to destroy a dishrag and a pencil. This was a freaking *boulder.*

116

"Running out of time, Nix." Ares leaned back against the farthest reaches of the boat. "Stretch forward so you can touch the boulder."

Shit, shit, shit.

The refrain wouldn't die.

But I did as he said, trying to keep most of my weight towards the bow of the boat so that the stern wouldn't sink beneath the surface. We couldn't just roll the boat out. If our weight didn't cause the stern to sink—and us with it—the boulder might tear the side of the hull.

The Vampire Court was really freaking clever.

Carefully, I propped my hand on the middle bench—the one where I sat when I rowed—and reached the other toward the rock. My fingertips brushed the rough surface and I called upon my new magic.

It was hard at first, and foreign. I had to force my mind to calm as I recalled destroying the pencil.

Wind.

I needed the wind. I focused on the feeling of the breeze against my face, drawing it within me. My head pounded as I let the breeze fill my body. I envisioned it destroying the rock, buffeting it to pieces. I fed it into the stone, forcing more and more power into the giant boulder that was threatening to take us to the bottom of the sea.

A sharp electric sting landed on my hand, breaking my concentration. Pain sang up my arm from where the jellyfish had landed, but I forced it away.

The wind.

I focused on the breeze, trying to ignore the searing pain, and fed my destructive magic into the boulder. A crack appeared down the middle. Hope flared in my chest.

I pushed more magic into it, giving it everything I had. My heart thundered and my vision dimmed, but I kept going.

More cracks formed in the rock, shooting down like lightning. The thing began to crumble, most of it disappearing before it hit the ground.

I gasped raggedly, trying to fill my lungs as I forced my magic into the rock. Slowly, so slowly, it crumbled away to dust.

As soon as it was gone, the stern popped up out of the water, sitting more naturally on the surface.

But water began to pour in through the holes created by the spikes on the bottom of the boulder. Gasping, exhausted from using the Destroyer magic, I conjured little rubber plugs. As fast as I could, I shoved them into the holes, stopping the flow of water.

Jellyfish stung me as I worked, pain racing through my body as they made contact. My vision swam, but I didn't quit till I'd finished.

Finally, the boat stopped leaking. I collapsed on the bench, drawing my legs up out of the water and trying to catch my breath.

"Good work, Nix," Ares said.

"Screw you." I surveyed the bottom of the boat, which was full of water and jellyfish. Fortunately not so much water that we were sinking. "You're the one who got me into this."

"You know that's not true."

"It's kinda true." I conjured a bucket, handing it to him. "Get to it."

He grinned and saluted, then began to bail out the boat, working carefully to avoid the jellyfish stings. All around us, the jellyfish in the sea had sunk back to the bottom, as if the challenge were over and they were on break.

I inspected my hands, which were bright red. It hurt just to flex my fingers, but it felt like the pain was fading at least a little.

"You were magnificent," Ares said. "But are your hands all right?"

"Just dandy." I tugged the map out of my pocket and studied it for clues.

Suddenly, I realized that it was in another language. I'd read it so easily and naturally that I'd just assumed it was English. The information had flowed into my brain like it wanted to be there.

But the map was written in a language I'd never seen before.

Shit. It was my Informa power, stolen from Aleric, that was giving me the ability to understand it. Informas could read any language.

I looked up at Ares, who was almost finished bailing out the boat. "You told them about the powers I stole."

CHAPTER NINE

Ares's green gaze met mine. "I didn't."

"Liar." I hadn't felt Doyen poking inside my mind for information like she'd done a few days ago at the warehouse where I'd first met her. Which meant he'd told the Court.

"No. I didn't have to tell them." His voice was sincere, his eyes honest. "They're not stupid, Nix. It was obvious that you'd take Aleric's power. Who wouldn't want to know the information he'd stolen?"

Damn it. Outsmarted by the vampires.

"You're testing my magic with this challenge," I said. "The magic I already had and the magic I've taken."

"Yes. We need to know that you can control it. That's part of the problem with FireSouls. If you can't control what you take, you're a liability."

"And that's why you insisted I practice."

He nodded. "It is. I want you to succeed."

"Big jump from destroying pencil to a boulder. I could have died if I'd failed."

"I knew you wouldn't fail. And I wouldn't let you die." He set the bucket down on the floor of the boat. All the jellyfish were gone. "But we need to keep going."

He gestured for me to move so that he could row, and I did. My hands were too beat up to keep going, and I'd need all the help I could get. Though I was pissed enough at him that I didn't want to accept his assistance, I wasn't dumb enough to look a gift horse in the mouth. And since this horse was offering free labor, I'd take it.

Ares picked up the oars and set back to work, pulling us through the water. I checked the compass, finding that he was going in the right direction.

"You know where we're going?" I asked.

"Just a good sense of direction."

"But there are no landmarks out here. And the moon is right above us."

"Like I said."

I scowled at his strong back. He was a damned enigma wrapped in a riddle or whatever. I'd thought it before and I'd probably think it again. I wanted to trust him—he'd helped me before and said he liked me—but he was on the Vampire Court, which was currently a giant pain in my butt.

Determined to get through this trial and back to solving the mystery of the stolen magical beaker, I inspected the map.

We were supposed to land on a shore, where we'd be greeted by someone—no idea who—and from them we'd learn about where we could spend the night.

The night? This was an overnight thing?

Though part of me was annoyed, more of me was grateful. We'd been rowing for hours, battling sea monsters, and I really could use a freaking nap. I spun around, hoping to see land.

For once, something went right. I could see the shore. It glittered like a pale rainbow, a thousand colors glinting in the moonlight. Past the beach, there were trees. Short, stunted things with silvery white bark and tiny leaves.

It was breathtaking.

"We're nearly there," I said.

Ares turned around, then grinned. "Good."

He put some more muscle into it, rowing us even faster toward the shore. I turned around, crouching in the bow so I didn't lose my footing when we beached.

Up close, the beach was even more beautiful. Tiny pebbles glittered white with the fire of rainbows within.

Opals. The beach was made of opals.

The bow plowed into the opal beach and I leapt out, then dipped down and picked up a handful. I held it out to Ares. "Is this how you're so rich? Your beaches are made of gemstones?"

"There's no shortage of valuable resources here." He jumped out of the boat and pulled it onto the shore.

I was about to demand more information—this beach was made of freaking gemstones!—when a rustling came behind me. A clattering sound, almost. Like someone was running on the beach.

I spun, guard up.

A small person charged me. But not a person. They glittered like the opals, all rainbows and sparkle.

I held up my hands. "We come in peace!"

Like a bunch of aliens?

I didn't have time to examine my ridiculous word choice. The opal monster, who was only about four and a half feet tall and had no facial features, plowed into me, throwing me back onto the ground.

I was too slow, too weak from the jellyfish. The creature plowed a fist into my gut. Pain flared and I *oofed* out a breath.

Shit!

This little guy was fighting dirty. I planted my hands on his— her?—chest and heaved, throwing him off me. I leapt on him, trying to pin him to the ground.

His flesh was hard as stone—too hard to punch, too hard to stab. He thrashed beneath me, stronger than I expected.

Beside me, Ares struggled with three of them, unable to hurt them because they were made of gemstone but also unable to completely throw them off.

"What the hell am I supposed to do?" I demanded.

"The map!" Ares threw off an opal monster as another charged him. "It told you!"

Shit, what had it said? That I'd meet someone who would give me information about finding a place to stay?

The opal creature with no face wasn't very friendly. And it didn't even have a freaking mouth! How was it going to give me directions?

It thrashed beneath me, landing a hard blow to my shoulder. My mind raced. I was supposed to use my new powers.

That made this pretty obvious.

But I'd never even tried to use the Informa gift. That magic had sat so easily and comfortably within me that I hadn't had to. I'd only practiced the Destroyer gift because the magic was making me sick.

But this was trial by fire. These little monsters weren't going to let up.

I strained to keep the opal creature immobilized while I searched my memory for what Cass had told me about using my Informa power. Thank fates I'd asked her to look into it.

I just had to touch him to suck the information right out of his head.

Creepy.

Invasive.

I really didn't like this.

The creature wiggled, freeing an arm and landing a punch to my side.

Oof.

Pain streaked through me. Getting punched by a rock hurt like hell.

I leaned heavily on the little creature and touched my hand to its head.

"Sorry about this," I muttered.

Unsure of what to do next, I decided to try just asking. "Where can we stay tonight?"

Information blared into my mind, pictures and words and sounds.

Holy crap! I heaved backward, too shocked to maintain contact.

"I got it!" I scrambled away from the creature, not wanting to attack or be attacked.

"Finally." Ares grunted and threw an opal monster off of him. "Pazūdi!"

I could read another language, but apparently I couldn't understand them when spoken. Whatever it was he'd said, the creatures froze, their heads turning toward Ares. They stopped their attack, then ran off, scampering towards the woods.

I scrambled to my feet, exhaustion weighing down my muscles, and turned to Ares. "What the hell was that?"

"Part of the challenge."

"Using my Informa gift." I scowled. "But you had control of them all the time."

"They obey the Vampire Court. Though it's their instinct to attack those on the opal beach to protect the stones, they'll stop if I tell them to."

"They're protecting the stones?"

"Yes. Otherwise this place would be mined to oblivion."

That'd be terrible. I was suddenly glad that Ares didn't get his wealth from here, while being simultaneously annoyed at his manipulation of the situation. I hated not being on the same side. He'd protect me and help me, but I never knew when he was orchestrating something. That opal creature had packed a hell of a punch. My side blazed in two places from his blows.

I turned and started toward the house I'd seen in my mind. Every step was exhausting.

Fortunately, the opal creature had given me directions as well as an image of the house. I was grateful to find that I'd only gotten the information I asked for—nothing more or less. I didn't want to know about that weird critter's sex life, for example.

Ares caught up quickly, his steps quiet on the beautiful beach. The place was magnificent. As we neared the trees, I caught sight of small furry creatures sitting on the branches. Black squirrels, with fur of obsidian and eyes that blazed a bright green.

"Night Terrors," Ares said.

"These little guys?"

I approached one, holding out a finger for the creature to sniff. It bared its teeth, revealing vampiric fangs. I jerked my hand back. "Okay, I get it."

The squirrel closed its mouth, looking cute as a button again. I turned to Ares. "Your world is weird."

"But wonderful. In a terrible way."

"Yes." I entered the forest, where the trees were short and twisted. They were only a few feet taller than me, their branches as thick around as my thigh and so gnarled that they looked to be thousands of years old.

"This forest is ancient, isn't it?" I said.

"Very. Thousands of years old."

I was careful not to touch the trees. Who knew what they had up their sleeve. Ancient creatures—even plants—knew how to protect themselves.

"How far are we?" Ares asked.

"Another ten minutes, I would guess."

We walked silently through the woods, weaving our way between the trees. The path was so narrow that Ares kept behind me.

When we came upon the cottage, I gasped. It was fairytale perfect, made of pale gray stone with a thatched roof and pink roses climbing up the sides. Upon further inspection, I realized that it was ramshackle, some of the glass windows cracked and the door hanging off its hinges.

"Have you ever been here?" I asked Ares.

"No. I've only been as far as the opal beach. But this place was once owned by a hermit who preferred the company of the Night Terrors. He left this realm about ten years ago."

I almost made a joke, but remembered Doyen and Magisteria. I might have preferred the Night Terrors, too, if they were my alternative.

I kept my senses alert as I approached the cottage, but all was quiet. The door opened easily. Moonlight filtered in, revealing a simple one-room space and the shadowy form of a couch across the way. A bed was pushed against the right wall, a kitchen against the left. Everything looked to be in pretty good shape, thank fates. Not a bad place to spend the night.

There was a table in the middle and a few candles sat on an iron plate. I approached, conjuring a match and lighting the three ivory candles.

They flared to life, brighter than normal candles. "Nice."

While Ares inspected the kitchen, I took stock of my situation. I was famished, filthy, and my whole body hurt.

First things first, then.

"Any food in there?" I asked.

"No." Ares turned to me, looking too big in the tiny cabin. It had not been built for a giant vampire enforcer.

"Hmm." I walked to the door, stepping out into the darkness. Maybe the hermit had had a garden. I could conjure some food, but I should start to save my magic. Who knew what Ares would throw at me. He might be acting like everything was normal, but I couldn't go on that alone.

I followed an overgrown path to the back yard, finding a wild vegetable garden. It was bordered on all sides by the stunted silvery trees, though a few of them looked like they might bear fruit.

I rooted around in the wild greenery until I found a few cucumbers. At the edge of the garden, one of the trees was dotted with fat apples. Though the bark was silver, the apples looked red and tasty.

Footsteps sounded behind me. I turned to see Ares. "Can I eat these?"

He nodded. "They're fine."

I pulled one off the tree and tossed it to him. "You first."

He grinned, though his eyes darkened, as if he were hurt that I didn't trust him.

That was weird.

But he should expect it. We weren't exactly in the easiest situation here.

Fortunately, he bit into the apple without hesitation. Good.

I pulled down a few more, then returned to the house with my loot. Ares had set a couple plates out on the table, so I conjured some big blocks of cheese, bread, and beef jerky. With the cucumbers and apples, it wasn't the worst meal.

Ares stepped through the door.

"It's your lucky day," I said. "Because I'm going to share."

"Is that just because you're worried about me biting you?" he asked.

"I considered it, sure." Ares was a vampire. When vampires got hungry, they got all vampy and bitey. Since I didn't need any of that business right now—or ever—it was definitely in my best interest to feed him.

"You know I won't bite you without your consent." His voice was dark. Rough.

"Why would I consent?" I sounded squeakier than I liked, that was for damned sure.

"You know why."

Oh, shit. I swallowed hard, my insides heating up embarrassingly. To distract myself, I grabbed an apple and chomped down. Tart sweetness exploded on my tongue.

Delicious.

I chowed through two apples, not even bothering to sit down, then moved onto the bread and cheese and jerky. I finished the meal with a cucumber. Ares had sat and was eating more slowly.

"Feel better?" he asked.

"Yeah." I looked around, searching for soap or a bathroom. There was nothing but an old bar of soap on the counter. "Do you think there's anywhere to get cleaned up?"

"Most cottages in the forest like this are built near rivers. That would do for a bath." He pointed to the right, which I thought was north. "There should be one a dozen yards that way. I thought I heard rushing water."

"Thanks. I'm going to get cleaned up."

"Stay alert."

I nodded and grabbed the bar of soap, then hurried out the door and toward the north, following the noise of the river that I could hear once I got a few yards from the house.

It was a beautiful sight, the water a deep blue that glinted under the light of the moon. Pale green ferns bordered the river, except for the area around a little pool formed by a rock wall. The river water flowed through it, creating a natural bathtub.

Jackpot.

I shrugged out of my dirty clothes and climbed gingerly into the pool. It was cool and perfect, an ideal temperature in the warm night air. I sank down until the water brushed my chin, sitting on a natural stone bench.

As I let the water soothe away some of my aches, I stared up at the moon. It was so bright that it was hard to see the stars, but I managed to pick out a few. Two bright red specks flew high overhead, glinting in the moonlight.

The Pūķis. Keeping me company. I grinned. Though I

couldn't see them clearly, I knew it was them. They must have flown around the giant silver lake.

"You seem to be spending a lot of time in our realm." The feminine voice made me pop up, my heart thundering.

I searched the forest, frantic to find the threat. I had so little magic left after the trials of today. And a fight? It'd be a tough one to win, given how I was feeling.

Laima sat on a rock across from me, one knee crossed over the other and her head propped on her hand. Her wild blond hair fell in tousles over the left side of her face and her red lips were pursed. She looked amazing.

No wonder Corbatt had lost his mind over her.

"Stalking me, much?" I asked.

Laima laughed. "That's no way to talk to a goddess."

"But it is a way to talk to a stalker."

Laima laughed again. She stood and magic swirled around her in silver sparkles, replacing her silver jumpsuit with a silver bikini.

She climbed into the water, taking the seat across from me. "I'm really old. The years get boring after a while, and you're a new person."

"Yeah, I can see how that might get boring. Being alive forever." I tried to relax against my seat, but it was tough.

Though she was friendly, and technically sharing my bath, power radiated from her. Her magical signature was off the charts, and there was something in her eyes that said *Don't fuck with me*.

Message received, goddess.

"So you're just here to chat?" I asked.

"Basically. This is normally Bridge night, but the other girls had to beg off. Too much ambrosia last night. They've got hangovers like you wouldn't believe."

"Gotcha."

"How are you enjoying our fair realm?" She waved a hand to indicate the scenery around us.

"Well, it's really pretty. But mostly it's just kinda tries to kill me a lot."

"I've been watching." Her brows rose. "But you've done well. You used a lot more magic this time."

"I had to. Part of the challenge."

"They're really putting you through the ringer. Doyen and Magisteria must not trust you."

"What about Ares?" He'd made it clear he didn't yet trust me.

"Oh, he does. Totally." Laima nodded knowingly. "I've been watching that one for years."

"Watching?"

"Oh yeah. For gods, spying is just like watching soaps. There's no TV here, unfortunately. What I get is through magical means, and the channels suck. So watching vampire machinations is half our entertainment."

"You and the other girls. Who are also goddesses?"

"Yep. Three of us are fate goddesses. There are some others as well. Harvest, Death, Courtship, and Chaos. We have a wine-and-spy night."

"Spy night. Not *spa* night?"

"Yeah. For spying. It's like humans getting together to watch the Bachelor. Except we only got two seasons of that and are desperate now. So we spy on the Vampire Court. Along with some of the nobility."

I grinned. I was in a magical hot tub, gossiping with a goddess about the Vampire Court? Score. "See anything good?"

"All the time. Magisteria has a *very* active love life. And Doyen isn't so bad either."

Right. She was most interested in girls. But what I wanted to know about wasn't Magisteria or Doyen. "What about Ares?"

Her eyes gleamed. "Oh, he's my favorite."

Okay, boys and girls for Laima. "Why?"

She tapped her chin. "That one is the puzzle. But it's clear he trusts you. And likes you."

"How can you tell? And what do you mean by puzzle?"

She shrugged a slender shoulder. "Well, he's all business. Warrior first, person second. A machine, almost. Ever since he came into his majority ten years ago, at eighteen, he's taken his role so seriously you'd think he was the god of Death."

"He's pretty serious?"

"As the grave."

I chuckled. I loved a bad pun. "Tell me more."

"Well, he spent most of his young adulthood chasing anything in a skirt." She held up a finger. "Not goddesses though. He's not an idiot. But he really seemed to enjoy life. People. Parties."

"And then?"

"Then he became the Enforcer. It changed him. The responsibility or something, I don't know. Hasn't shown interest in having a life since." She scoffed. "Much to our dismay, as I'm sure you can imagine. That's one whole part of the Vampire Court with very little drama."

"So he just works and that's it."

"Until you." Laima pointed at me. "I've seen him break the rules for you."

"Like healing me at the volcano?"

"And giving you hints today." She tsked. "He's *never* done that before."

Hmmm. My heart fluttered. *Settle down, you.* "So, what? Do you think I can trust him?"

She shrugged again. Her signature move, I'd guess. For a fate goddess, she was pretty good at giving unclear signals. "I think there's a good chance you can. He's treated you like no one else in the ten years since he's changed. Something about you, maybe."

"That's crazy."

"I don't know. You seem pretty great. You're special, Nix."

I blushed. A hot goddess was flirting with me?

I'd take it! My ego could use the boost. And maybe I was just making it up. But whatever.

"Do you have any advice for completing the task ahead?" I asked.

"Stick with Ares. It's not over yet. And it's not going to get any easier."

I wasn't surprised to hear it. Not like I was surprised to hear her back Ares up. The reserved vampire was such a mystery.

"Well, I'd better get going or I'll turn into a prune." Laima climbed out of the hot tub. "See you soon."

She disappeared before I could ask what she meant.

Dang. But it was time to get out. I didn't want Ares getting worried and coming after me.

My mind stutter-stopped. Why did I assume he'd be worried about me at all? That he cared?

Probably because of what Laima had said. And what he himself had said about liking me. And he had helped me out. Maybe I needed to get over my own wariness.

I reached for the soap and scrubbed up, washing away the dirt and doing a mediocre job of cleaning my hair. My muscles still ached and my hands hurt from the jellyfish stings, but it was a lot better than it had been.

Finally clean, I climbed out of the water. I debated a while about whether or not to conjure clean clothes and settled on expending enough energy for socks, underwear, and T-shirt. This time, I chose a Xena Warrior Princess cat shirt. She was a badass warrior—in feline form.

The forest was quiet as I made my way back to the cottage. Ares was inside, crouched near the hearth. A small fire burned inside. His hair was damp.

"Did you take a bath, too?" I asked.

He nodded, rubbing a hand through his wet hair. "Farther down the river."

I sure hoped he hadn't heard anything that Laima had said.

"So, we've got until tomorrow morning before this thing starts up again?"

"Yeah."

"And I can sleep. Without worrying that something will jump out at me." I tapped my chin. "Specifically, I'm thinking squid or other many-armed creatures."

"No more many-armed creatures. Not for tonight." He crossed his heart. "On my honor."

And I believed him. I was waffling on trust a lot these days, but I believed him in this.

"Then I'm hitting the hay. Dibs on the bed." I left him with the couch which was probably too short, but I was mercenary. I wanted to survive this.

"Sure." He walked to the table and picked up some leaves. "But first, these. For your hands."

He crossed the room toward me, holding out the slender green stalks. My heart warmed.

"Arrowreed? Where'd you find it?" The slender green plants soothed burns and other wounds and even had some healing properties.

"By the river. I thought you might want it."

"Thanks." I thought of what Laima had said about him being solely dedicated to his work these past ten years. But here he was, thinking of my wounds and scavenging for helpful herbs.

"Hold out your hands," he said.

My gaze darted to his, then I followed his instructions, holding out my hands with the backs facing up. The wounds were the worst there, particularly on the right hand, where one of the jellyfish had landed a direct hit.

Tension thrummed across my skin as I stood still, watching Ares break the end off of one of the delicate reeds. He used it like a paintbrush, swiping the clear fluid over my wounds.

His touch was delicate as a butterfly's, the soothing gel leaving comfort in its wake.

"Turn them over." His voice was rough.

Suddenly, heat flared inside me. He was standing *so* close. I could smell the chill winter air of his magic and the warmer scent that was distinctly him, freshly clean from the river. I sucked it into my lungs, trying to be subtle but unable to help myself.

Ares painted the gel over my palms, his hands steady and calm. Soon, the pain had diminished to almost nothing, which left more space for me to focus on what it felt like to stand so close to Ares. While he was taking care of me.

It was heady stuff, making my mind buzz and my body warm.

"Lift your head."

I jumped slightly, and did as I was told, lifting my chin and tilting my head so that he could get to the jellyfish sting on my neck.

My gaze met his, just briefly, and the heat in his eyes made me swallow hard.

Apparently he was just as affected by the closeness as I was. And maybe, just maybe, he liked taking care of me.

My gaze darted away—pure self-preservation—and he applied the gel to my neck, painting the clear fluid on with a delicate touch. After a moment, it felt good. Delicate sweeps of the brush that made me think of other things. Hotter things.

Then it was over.

He lowered the Arrowreed. I looked at him.

"Better?" he asked.

"Much."

His hot gaze traced my features. The muscles at his neck tensed, just slightly, and I realized that his hands were fisted. As if he wanted to touch me, but didn't dare.

"You've done well in the challenges, Nix."

"Thanks," I whispered.

The tension between us—pure chemistry—crackled in the air. It was electrifying, as if we were connected by invisible threads that struck with delicious energy every time either of us so much as breathed or shifted.

An image of me kissing him flashed in my mind. I could just wrap my arms around his neck and press my lips to his. Taste him and feel him and just *be* with him.

I'd leaned in and almost raised my arms before I realized how dumb that was.

This was a terrible time. And considering that I didn't know if I could trust him—there was probably never going to be a good time.

I stepped back, face flushed and body going wild.

Down girl.

Ares stepped back, face suddenly shuttered. All the heat was gone, except for the tiniest banked fire in his eyes that he couldn't hide.

That was some small satisfaction for my frustrated self. He *did* want me. A lot. This cold, quiet man who'd given up girls after he'd joined the Vampire Court.

But he wasn't going to make the first move.

And it was so clear why. His role in the Vampire Court put him in a position of power over me. And he wouldn't abuse that.

I liked that as much as I hated it.

But I'd think about it later.

"Thanks for the Arrowreed." The words came out scratchy, as if my throat wasn't ready to break the quiet spell over us.

"No problem." He put the unused reeds on the table.

"I don't remember seeing any of that by the river." And I usually had a really great eye for this stuff.

"I didn't say I got it from *this* river."

"So you went far away for it? Teleporting?"

He smiled, and it was kinda... gentle. "Do you need all the details?"

"I guess not." I knew enough anyway. It was enough to warm my heart. Unable to just stand here staring at him, I turned and went to the bed. I'd just gotten under the covers and tugged off my jeans when he spoke.

"How did you get the name Phoenix?" he asked.

I yawned. "Gave it to myself."

"Why?"

"I liked it."

"That can't be all there is to it."

I leaned up, eyeing him. He lay on the couch, arm behind his head. "Why are you so interested?"

He shrugged. "You're interesting."

"Hmm."

"People don't just name themselves Phoenix without a reason."

I sighed. Could I trust him? Laima seemed to think so. And it couldn't hurt to tell him something that was in the past.

"I don't remember my life before I was fifteen. Just snippets I've gotten from dreams. I had a good family, I think. But when I was fourteen, I was abducted by a man I called the Monster. He wanted to make me a slave—force me to use my FireSoul powers to serve him."

Ares's hands formed fists and his brows dropped low over his eyes. "What happened to him?"

"He's dead now. Don't worry about him." Just the thought of him being gone forever was enough to make my heart calm and joyous. "But when I escaped, I was fifteen. I had no memories. I just woke in a field, looking up at the stars. And I named myself for the constellation."

"Not just for the constellation," Ares said. "Your past was rubble. A nightmare you couldn't remember. But you planned to rise again, greater than before."

Tears pricked my eyes. My throat tightened. It took all I had to squeeze out a tight, "Yeah."

"You're impressive, Phoenix Knight."

"Thanks." I swallowed hard, clearing my throat. "Why are you so serious all the time? Do you like being the Enforcer?"

I didn't explicitly mention what Laima had said, but he got my drift.

"I do," he said. "I wasn't always this serious. In fact, I didn't want to be the Enforcer when I was young. But when my father died—it was terrible. He'd protected us for so long, and then he was just gone."

"How did it happen?"

"He was hunting a murderer. A particularly violent one. He was ambushed. Never saw it coming." His voice sounded tight. Pained.

"That had to be hard. To sneak up on a guy like him, I mean."

"Nearly impossible." Ares's gaze was dark as he studied the ceiling above his head. No doubt he was seeing memories he didn't like. "A friend betrayed him. It was the only way they got the drop on him."

"So you avenged his murder." It was so obvious.

"I did. But I had to change everything about myself to do it. Become stronger, quieter, more ruthless. My father was full vampire. I am not. I had to overcome that weakness."

"But isn't it a strength, since it gives you greater magical powers?"

"Some might see it that way. But a vampire's ruthlessness—the ruthlessness that overcomes me when I'm in this realm—that's key to the job."

"So you changed everything about yourself and succeeded."

"Eventually. And now I do what I do."

"And you spend as little time as possible in this realm."

The corner of his mouth kicked up in a sexy smile. "That's for my sanity."

It was stupid of me not to trust this man—at least with information about the men who'd killed Marin. I needed to catch those guys—for so many reasons. And Ares was the perfect person to help.

"Have you learned anything more about the people who arranged for Aleric to kill Marin?" I asked.

"Why are you interested?" he asked.

I leaned up and met his gaze. "It has to do with the Triumvirate thing that Laima was talking about the other day."

"Which you never explained."

"I'll explain more if you tell me something good."

He nodded. "Fine. We've learned that Marin's death was arranged by a man who leads an international criminal organization."

"Do you know anything about him?"

"He's powerful. He has connections in Europe and Asia. Black magic connections. We're trying to sort them out now."

That would explain the magical enchantments protecting his compound in Magic's Bend. "Are you trying to catch him?"

"We haven't yet found him, but we have some clues. And yes, we're trying to catch him. Marin's death cannot go unpunished."

"But you don't know why he killed Marin. At least, what the information was that he sought."

"No, but you do." His serious gaze met mine. "And I'm hoping you'll tell me."

Understanding dawned. "Hey, whoa. Have you been waiting this out? Giving me time to tell you what I know?"

Was he running a long-con on me—gaining my trust until I confessed all—or being nice and giving me time to tell him?

"Basically," he said. "You needed to complete the trials. The court demanded it. But you also have information that will help us. It's one of the reasons we'd rather be your allies than your enemy. And we don't force our allies to tell us things."

"Instead, you're slowly gaining my trust. While torturing me with these trials."

"I admit, it's a bit Machiavellian. But we really do need to know that you're not a corrupt FireSoul. And that you can handle your powers. I now believe you can. Doyen and Magisteria will come around, too."

"And then?"

"And then, we work together to help each other. We protect you if the need arises—from any threat, including the Order of the Magica. And if you have information that will help us find the man truly responsible for Marin's death, then you tell us. Symbiotic. Allies."

I lay down and stared at the ceiling. He had a point. And though it was twisty and cunning, it was also very honest. "Okay. That could work. Sounds reasonable."

Exhaustion pulled at me, reminding me that I'd had a hell of a day.

"What is the information that Aleric was after, then?" he asked.

"Dragons," I said.

Shock covered his face, making his brows rise and his lips part. "Are you serious? But they're gone."

I shrugged "The only thing that I understood were the words 'dragons' and 'returned.' The rest was encrypted a long time ago by the Cathar Perfecti."

"When we were there, they said they coded the secret," Ares said.

"Exactly. I'd like to ask them what the code is, but I doubt they'll tell us."

"Perhaps we can try later. Do you know if Aleric passed the information onto his boss?"

"No idea. If so, hopefully he hasn't broken the code yet."

"We can only hope." I yawned hard, my eyes closing against my will. I could feel Ares's desire to ask me more questions—and maybe even his desire for something else, like a tension on the air —but all he said was, "Get some sleep."

After everything I'd been through, it was easy to oblige.

CHAPTER TEN

We woke early the next morning, which felt weird, since it was still dark. Honestly, I had no idea it was morning except for the fact that I was awake.

While Ares woke, I went to the back garden to collect more apples.

There was another moon in the sky, this one slightly larger. At least, I thought it was larger. The silvery forest surrounding the cabin seemed a bit brighter, at least. And I could see the Pūķis better. They flew high above the house and I was certain they were keeping an eye on me.

Maybe it was fanciful, but I didn't care.

I was pulling one of the shiny red fruits off the tree when the magic in my comms charm ignited.

"Nix?" Del's voice was quiet but clear.

"Hey!" I tucked the apple into the bowl I'd found in the house.

"How's it going with the challenges?" Cass asked.

"Fine." Surviving Kraken, chilling with a goddess. All in a day's work. "Hopefully done today."

"Good," Del said. "Because we may have found a way into the compound."

"And it's not going to be easy," Cass said.

"What is it?"

"We've got to go by sea. No way to get through the enchantments on the fence that surrounds the land portion. Or the guards. The sea is our only bet."

"Damn." My recent experience traveling via water had not gone well.

"We'll do a bit more recon today, hopefully find out a bit more," Del said. "But right now, it's looking like we'll be doing a water approach."

"Learn anything else?" I asked.

"Definitely the dragon gang and not a coincidence. We've now seen ten with the marking."

"Geez." I stared down at the apples. "Not ideal."

"Nope!" Cass said. "But we'll let you know if we learn anything more. Be careful, okay?"

"Yeah," Del said. "Watch your back. We don't want anything happening to you."

"Thanks guys. Good luck at the compound. And *don't* go in without me."

"We won't," Cass said. "And we'll be fine. We're bringing Claire for backup. She's good at these kinds of things."

"Excellent. Talk to you later. Love you."

"Love you back," they both said.

We cut the connection. I grabbed one more apple, then headed into the house. Fortunately, my magic was feeling rejuvenated after my sleep. Having to recharge was annoying, but at least I'd managed it.

Ares looked up from where he knelt by the fire, stoking the flames. "Were you talking outside?"

"Just to my friends." I pointed to the comms charm. "Just letting them know how it was going."

I handed him the apples and conjured some more bread and cheese. We dug in, finishing our breakfast in record time, enjoying the heat of the fire. Though it wasn't freezing outside, the morning was damp.

"Ready to get a move on?" I asked.

As much as I dreaded what was to come, I wanted to get back to my *deirfiúr* and help them figure out the mystery of the dragon gang and the stolen beaker.

"Sure." He brushed off his hands and stood.

I grabbed the rest of the healing Arrowreed off the table, shoved it into my pocket, then led the way outside. I pulled the map out and consulted it for the twelfth time. I'd figured out my next move earlier this morning, but I just wanted to double check.

"We'll go left, back around the cabin and through the woods," I said.

"Lead on."

Ares and I walked single file through the forest, once again constrained to the narrow path. We shouldn't have to leave it, according to the map. Normally, I'd be grateful. But the Vampire Court had a way of putting nasty surprises on their route.

As we walked, the Night Terrors leapt from silvery tree branch to silvery tree branch, keeping an eye on us. There were a lot of them—enough that should they decide to mount a coordinated attack, it'd become a real pain in the butt.

We walked for what felt like hours, weaving our way through the forest under the watchful gaze of the Night Terrors. Overhead, the two Pūķi swept through the sky, accompanying us. At least, I liked to think so. Eventually, they were joined by more, tiny red specs in the sky, their red wings illuminated by the light of the huge moon.

I'd almost relaxed by the time the shriek tore through the air.

My gaze darted around. "What the hell was that?"

Ares pointed right. "Sounds like it came from over there."

"Off the path." We weren't supposed to deviate from the path. The directions were very clear.

The shriek sounded again—this time, clearly distressed.

I looked up, searching for the Pūḳis. There were four above. Hadn't there been five before?

Another shriek.

The hair on my arms stood on end. My heart raced. I turned to Ares. "Something is wrong."

He stood alert, his body tense. He nodded.

The shrieks were clearly coming from the forest off the path. They weren't part of my challenge. But I couldn't just *ignore* them.

"Come on." I stepped off the path, my feet crunching against the leaves, and hurried toward the distressed cries.

Ares followed, keeping close behind me as we wove through the silvery trees in search of the distressed sounds. My heart pounded as a I ran, worry fueling my pace.

Ahead, the forest cleared. There were no trees, just a mass of strange green vines. The pile was about fifty feet across and rose like a small hill. It looked like a plate of giant alien spaghetti.

Fates, the vampire realm was weird. "What the hell is that?"

Ares stopped beside me. "Acid vines."

In the middle, something moves. A flash of red. Moments later, a surge of movement. A Pūḳi!

"He's trapped in the vines!" I pointed.

The Pūḳi was struggling to break free, flying for the sky only to be grabbed by the vines and pulled back down. Another red dragon flew through the sky, diving and darting, blowing his flame on the vines to free his friend.

But every time he got close and shot a blast of flame, the vine shot a neon green liquid at him. The dragon hissed and darted away, as if the liquid pained him.

Ares sighed, sadness in the sound. "Acid vines are the number one predator of Pūḳis."

I turned to Ares, fear pounding in my chest. "What do you mean?"

"They'll exhaust him by letting him escape, then catching him again. Once he can no longer move, they'll slowly eat him."

Horror opened a hole in my chest. "No." I turned back to the pit of vines. "I'm going to go get him."

"You can't. They'll do the same to you."

"I don't care." I conjured a sword. "I'll cut them off."

Ares shook his head, eyes serious. Angry, almost. "Don't. The vines are filled with acid. It'll burn your skin right off."

So if I couldn't cut them and they'd capture me like that Pūķi, I was screwed. But the Pūķi shrieked and struggled, trying to escape.

"I'm not leaving him." My mind raced. There was no way in hell I could just walk away and keep going on my task for the Vampire Court.

"It's nature. The acid vines must eat, just like anything. Like a bobcat must eat a rabbit. That's the way nature is." But sadness glinted in his eyes.

He hated this.

I knew it as much as I knew that I hated it.

"I *know* it's nature." And he was right—hard shit like this happened all the time out in the wild. I loved snakes and mice both, but snakes couldn't live without eating mice. Didn't mean I liked it. "But the Pūķis are my friends."

"There's nothing you can do." Ares's voice was hard, but sad. "You must continue the task. Let's go back."

But there was something else on his face—something I couldn't really identify. Encouragement? Expectation?

I didn't have time to decipher his strange moods. That Pūķi was getting weaker and I'd wasted enough time already.

There were no trees near enough that I could tie a rope to, so I couldn't swing my way to the Pūķi. Nor was I skilled enough to conjure a flying device other than a hang glider, and there wasn't enough wind for that. I wished I could conjure liquid nitrogen to freeze them, but chemicals like that were time consuming to conjure.

My sword was the only defense I could think of, and I couldn't let that acid debilitate me, so I quickly conjured a pair of tough leather pants, gloves, and a welding mask. My leather jacket and boots would protect the rest of me.

I hoped.

I tugged it on quickly, not sparing a glance for Ares, then raced toward the pit of vines.

Fates, this was possibly dumb.

But the Pūķi's cries drove me forward. I prayed the momentum would keep me going. I charged through the vines. It worked—for a while.

I dodged and raced and stomped, avoiding the biggest vines. Small ones wrapped around my ankles, but I broke through them by the sheer force of my run.

Acid sprayed from them when they broke, splattering on my pants. I could hear the acid hissing slightly as it burned its way through.

I was halfway to the Pūķi by the time the first of the acid ate through my leather pants and then through my jeans. The burn made my eyes tear and sweat break out on my skin.

I flinched and kept running, but the vines were becoming thicker as I neared the middle. I tried leaping over one that lay like a log beneath the rest, but another vine caught me around the thigh.

I sliced through it with my sword, watching in horror as thick green liquid spilled from the severed vine. I dodged away from it, but some splattered on my thigh. It was so much that it quickly ate through the double layer of fabric.

Shit! That hurt.

I struggled away, limping and clawing my way through the vines that were now up to my thighs. My lungs burned and my heart thundered.

The Pūķi was still a good fifteen feet from me. So far.

I twisted to slice at a slender vine that had wrapped around my waist. As I severed it, I caught sight of Ares. Despite my mask, his expression was torn but so clear. His tortured eyes, crumpled brow, fisted hands, and warrior's posture. He even had his shadow sword gripped in his hand, though he didn't seem to notice that he'd even conjured it.

He wanted to dive into the vines, but clearly felt he shouldn't.

It was so weird, but I *really* didn't have time to mull it over. A vine wrapped around my arm, squeezing tight. I hacked it away, flinching as a tiny droplet of acid hit my neck in the space where the mask joined my jacket collar.

The vines kept coming, more and more. Soon, I was slicing left and right, acid spraying. There were too many, and they were strong. One smacked the blade from my hand.

Fear stole my breath.

Before I could conjure another, a huge vine had grabbed me around the waist, twisting me around and dragging me down. Ares's roar of frustration and rage rent the air. Through a gap in the vines, I caught sight of him charging in.

Would he fare any better than me, though?

Not that it mattered. I tried to shove aside the fear that tightened my muscles. I'd never waited for a guy to rescue me before and I wasn't about to start now. I struggled and strained.

No way I could use a sword—not when I was nearly covered in the vines. I'd drown in the acid that they would bleed. And *screw that.*

My mind raced. What else could I use? My magic wasn't second nature. Just the conjuring. Could I destroy the vine? Did that power even work on living things?

I doubted it—almost hoped it didn't because I didn't want to have a killing power, even though I needed it—but I tried anyway.

Calming my panicked mind enough to find the Destroyer

magic was nearly impossible, but I managed. As I worked, I caught brief glimpses of Ares hacking his way toward us.

He was faster than me—massively so. But the vines were too much even for him. They dragged at his limbs, slowing him.

The vines suffocated any wind that I might be able to feel on my face, so I had to imagine it within me, creating it from nothing but hope and fear. I forced the Destroyer magic into the vines. I could feel it within me, flowing out into the plants.

But it didn't flow into them. Almost like it was blocked. They kept crushing and writhing, encapsulating me evermore.

Suddenly, I couldn't breathe. They were squeezing too tightly. There were too many. I struggled and strained, trying to break my way free.

It did no good.

A hand appeared around a vine, pulling it away from my chest. I sucked in a ragged breath, finally able to breathe. My head cleared.

Through the vines, I could see Ares face. It was strained, his brow creased.

"I can do—"

A thick vine twined around Ares's neck, cutting off his breathing. Another around his head.

This was it. He was done for. I almost was.

But tearing the vine away from my chest gave me a chance. Enough breath that I could try this. I sucked in air, calling upon my Destroyer magic and forcing it into the plant. Again, it stopped dead, unable to penetrate.

Panic flared, whiting out my mind.

But the strangest thing happened.

I could suddenly *feel* the vines. Like I was connected to them. As if I'd opened a connection when I'd tried to force the Destroyer magic into them.

And now I could feel them. Like they were part of me, almost.

Release me. I forced my will into the vines, commanding them to loosen their grip. They resisted for a moment, pushing back at me. I could feel it in my mind, as the plants tried to force their will on me.

I focused, strengthening my resolve. They would not win.

The cries of the Pūķi helped give me strength. I couldn't let him down. Or Ares. Or myself. I didn't want to die in the vampire realm, eaten by acid vines.

Release us. I repeated the thought, envisioning the vines following my will.

Eventually, they relaxed, slowly loosening their grip.

I scrambled free, climbing over the biggest vines and frantically searching around me.

To my left, the Pūķi shot out of the vines, flying high for the sky. They didn't follow him.

I whooped with joy.

A rustling sounded from behind me. I spun. Ares climbed out from beneath some particularly huge vines. His neck burned red with an acid wound and his forearm looked like it'd been splashed badly as well.

"Are you okay?" I climbed toward him.

"Are you?" Worry colored his eyes, fear stark.

"Yeah. Let's get out of here." I scrambling toward the edge of the acid vines. They lay still and dormant beneath me, like the limp green spaghetti they'd first reminded me of. High above us, the Pūķis swooped and dived happily blowing fire from their noses.

By the time we stumbled away from the vines, my wounds were really hurting. I dragged myself far enough away that the vines couldn't bother me if they woke again, and sat at the base of one of the silver trees.

Ares stumbled down next to me, turning and taking off my mask, inspecting the wound at my neck. Worry gleamed in his eyes.

"How is it?" he asked.

"Fine." My wounds burned as I pulled off my leather jacket, gloves, and the extra pants that I'd conjured. The movement made pain flare, my acid wounds twinging as my skin pulled.

"Let me help you." Ares raised his wrist, as if he'd bite it.

"No." I held up a hand. My wounds hurt, but I did *not* need another connection to him.

"Let me."

"No." I dug the leftover Arrowreed out of my pocket and squeezed the gelatinous insides onto the wound on my thigh, which was the worst one. Immediately, the pain faded. The skin began to heal—not as well as it did when I used my special potion, but it would get me through the challenge until I could get a healer. I used the rest of the Arrowreed on my smaller burns, then shifted, still able to move fully. I could keep fighting on like this. It was a little painful, but fine.

Ares sighed. "You were impressive. How'd you get the vines to release us?"

"I don't know." And it was the honest truth. I had no freaking clue. I'd never used my FireSoul gift to take a plant magic from someone before. Hell, I'd never even *heard* of this kind of magic. I turned to Ares, whose neck and arm wounds were already healing.

He'd risked his life for me. Had he known he was doing that? That the vines were so strong? I stuffed the thought to the back of my mind, more concerned with the ramifications of what had just happened.

"Was that part of the Vampire Court challenge?"

He frowned, anger in his face, then nodded. "It wasn't supposed to be."

"Wasn't?"

"I insisted they not use this idea. Not sacrifice the Pūķi. But they did what they wanted." His voice vibrated with tightly controlled rage.

"What was the purpose?" I hadn't been able to use my

Destroyer magic there. And Ares had had no idea I'd possessed a plant magic, so they couldn't be testing that.

Ares looked up at the Pūķi. I followed his gaze.

"You can't guess what they were testing?" Ares said.

I watched the Pūķis, frowning. They looked so happy. I hated the idea of them in trouble. Understanding dawned. "They wanted to see what I would do when one of my friends was in danger."

He nodded. "You formed a bond with the Pūķi. They helped you at the volcano. They wanted to see if you would help them."

"And if I did, then I'd help you, my allies."

"That was the idea."

I frowned, not liking where this was going. "But what would have happened to the Pūķi if I'd failed? This challenge was nearly impossible."

"Exactly what you dreaded." He scrubbed a hand over his face, anger fading to ire. "I did not like this challenge. But Doyen and Magisteria insisted. I thought I'd talked them away from using it at all."

Something simmered within me, hot and angry. "The challenge was nearly impossible."

I'd defeated it only by using a magic I had no idea existed—which was *insane*. New magical talents didn't just pop up. You were born with them or you took them. You didn't spontaneously develop them, like growing a second head. And without him—I may not have managed it at all. "Did Doyen and Magisteria really expect me to succeed?"

Ares scrubbed a weary hand over his face. Suddenly, it was easy to see how this role tore him in two. He clearly did not like the machinations. He was too upfront for that.

"So they didn't expect me to succeed," I said.

"It's the reason I tried to convince them—threaten them—away from using this trial. It's the fact that you tried to save the Pūķi that counts, but sacrificing an innocent like that…"

"Monsters," I hissed.

"Yes, sometimes." His gaze met mine. "But when you went in to save the Pūķi, I knew you'd succeed. I didn't know how, just that you would."

"It's why you waited before coming in—" I remembered how torn his gaze was, how he'd so clearly wanted to charge in "—to give me a chance to win it according to their terms."

"It'd serve them right," he said. "It's part of a power play. You'd pass the test, but know that they could threaten those you love. We're allies, but there are still power games."

"The kind you don't like."

He scrubbed a hand over his face and nodded. "Exactly. But when you saved the Pūķi, you got one over on them."

I sat back against the tree, stunned at how twisty and dark their minds were. These games...

"And you broke the rules when you thought I was going to die under the vines. So you helped me."

"Technically, I failed."

"No, you didn't. If you hadn't pulled that vine away, I'd have suffocated before finding my power." I swallowed hard, meeting his gaze.

It was finally time to put my distrust to bed. He played both sides of the fence. He was on the Vampire Court and there was no getting away from it. But when it'd come time to declare an allegiance—he *had*. To me. When he'd entered the challenge and torn that vine away, he'd made himself very clear.

I reached for his hand, squeezing. "Thanks. You saved me."

"You saved yourself. I just helped a bit."

I could feel the small smile tug at my lips, but I forced it away. I didn't have time for happiness or tenderness. We needed to finish this.

I stumbled to my feet. "Let's go. I want to get this over with."

Ares stood, his wounds nearly closed.

I turned. "Come on."

I started through the forest, heading back to the path. Ares followed.

As we walked the Pūķis flew overhead, following us. They flew lower now, just over the trees. In the moonlight, they glinted red and bright.

They were our guardians.

Which proved to be true, when the trees began to whip their branches at us, slicing through the air and colliding with my arm.

"Shit!" I jumped away, clutching my injured arm.

Another branch whipped out, but a Pūķi dived, shooting fire at the tree. The branch retracted, not striking.

I smiled at the Pūķi. "Thanks."

The words had barely left my lips when two more branches struck out. But more Pūķis dived, shooting their fire at the trees. Soon, the Pūķis were on all sides, defending us from the attacking branches

"It looks like your friends appreciate your effort," Ares said.

"I appreciate theirs."

Getting through the forest was easy after that. The Pūķis defended us from the trees and then from the Night Terrors, who launched an attack from the branches.

I looked up when I'd heard a rustling branch. A fluffy black Night Terror was about to land on my head when a Pūķi roared. I swear the Night Terror wheeled in the air and turned, landing on the ground and streaking away.

The other Night Terrors—there were at least a hundred of them in the branches around, ready to leap upon us—hissed and darted away.

"Thanks, Pūķis." I gave them a thumbs-up. I did not want to fight a hundred little Night Terrors. No doubt a few of them would get their teeth into me, and no doubt they'd aim for arteries.

Man, I hoped these trials were almost over. I was exhausted and burned and I still had a stolen magical beaker and mob boss to deal with. At least I hadn't gotten sick from my Destroyer magic since I'd last used it.

Ahead of us, the forest thinned. Magic sparked on the air, something stronger than I was used to. Not a protective charm. But something else. A warning.

Don't mess with us.

But who was us?

"Are we getting close?" I consulted the map. We were near the X. Please let the X be the true end to this miserable adventure.

We passed between the thinning trees. Ahead of us, a hill rose gently toward the sky. It was topped by a white castle that looked like every fairytale castle rolled into one. It glinted in the moonlight, as if the thing were made of mirrors instead of impossibly white stone.

It was beautiful and terrifying at once. And without a doubt, it was my end destination.

CHAPTER ELEVEN

I laughed low. "I find your fairytale architecture to be a bit disturbing when contrasted against all of the miserable monsters you have lurking in your lakes and forests."

"Fairytales were full of horrible monsters."

I grinned at him. "Fair enough."

When I turned back to the white castle, I noted that it flew three pennants from the top three towers. The towers were all equally tall, and the pennants glowed gold, silver, and opal.

"Any hint on who lives there?" I asked.

Ares shook his head.

"No problem." *Bring it, vampire Bitches.*

I climbed up the hill, gaze riveted to the castle. The Pūķis flanked me, three on either side. They glowed red in the moonlight, fierce and loyal.

The castle gate was a massive wooden affair decorated with iron spikes. I stopped in front of it and shouted, "Might as well let me in!"

The gate creaked down, lowering over a moat filled with blue water glittering in the moonlight. It was so clear that I could see straight down. It was so deep that it looked bottomless.

"Those waters will suck you down to the middle of the earth," Ares said.

I gulped. "So stick to the bridge. Cool."

The bridge in question lowered fully to the ground. I drew in a deep breath and stepped on it, crossing into a massive courtyard filled with night-blooming flowers. Deep reds and blues and purples spilled from baskets and pots that decorated every surface and inch of wall.

The magic that vibrated on the air was stronger here, and somewhat familiar. The feeling of crashing waves, the sound of thunder, and an electric shock. There were more signatures that I couldn't identify, and they were powerful.

Overhead, the Pūķis circled the castle courtyard, their gazes on me. One dived, trying to reach me, but bounced off an invisible shield.

Suddenly, nerves prickled along my skin. Whoever was here didn't want me to have my dragon backup.

This place might be beautiful, but it was dangerous. Like Nightshade, one of my favorite poisonous plants. I turned to look at Ares, whose muscles were tense and his face set. He knew where we were, and he wasn't a fan.

I straightened my shoulders and walked through the courtyard. The map had stopped at the X, so I had no idea what I'd find. The uncertainty made my skin prickle with nerves, but I doubted I'd have to wait long.

Across the courtyard, the main keep rose four stories tall with wide blue doors. The blue was pale with silver filigree overtop—strange and delicate. The doors were basically a neon sign, I figured, so I walked toward them. Ares stayed at my side, his stride confident and his gaze alert.

He'd been here before, and despite his confidence, he was still a touch wary. Alert, more than anything.

Whatever made the vampire Enforcer wary definitely made me jumpy. Especially considering the powerful magic that imbued this place. It was in the air, the walls, the floor. Everywhere.

I reached the doors on the other side of the courtyard. Both doors swung open, as if expecting me. Despite their elegant appearance, they were six inches thick and strong enough to keep out a charging elephant.

Magic rolled out of the room, so powerful that I stumbled back. It felt like waves crashed into me as thunder vibrated in my chest and electricity flowed through my limbs.

I staggered, reaching out to hold the door as I swayed on my feet. It took everything I had to remain standing. My muscles shook from the magical energy, my bones trembled.

I'd never felt anything like this.

And yet, it was slightly familiar.

I glanced at Ares, who'd planted his feet and withstood the barrage. "You could have warned me."

"They like to make an impression," he said.

"They?"

"You'll see."

I sucked in a breath and walked through the doors, heart pounding in my throat. I kept my magic close to the surface, ready to go. In the face of such great power, I wasn't sure what I could do. But I'd have to at least try.

The room within was massive—the ceiling was four stories above and painted a pale blue with glittering silver stars. But it was the three thrones across the huge room that caught my eye.

Each held a woman. One was dressed in gold, another in silver, and the last in opal. Upon closer inspection, their clothes were actually armor.

And one of the women was Laima!

But she was far different, this version of Laima. With her delicate opal armor and hair done up in wicked braids, she looked like a warrior of old. Like if this were a movie, she'd fly into battle from high off the right screen, sword raised to behead some hapless fool.

Corbatt had been way out of his element.

And so was I.

Because Laima's power was now ten times what it had been, crashing over me like a tidal wave, and her eyes were all business. Gone was the gossipy woman in the hot tub—honestly, I'd think I'd imagined it. This Laima was terrifying. The kind of fate goddess who threatened to cut the thread of your life with one snip of her golden scissors.

Or battle axe, in the case of Laima. It rested against her throne, looking like it could behead giants. Opals decorated the shaft, just like her armor. Though it all looked delicate and lovely, strength radiated from it. Magic that would repel the attack of another. It prickled against my skin.

Worse, the two women next to her looked cold as ice and just as powerful. The crashing wave magic belonged to Laima, but the thunder and electricity belonged to the others.

One was dark-haired and dark-skinned, her golden armor shining in the light. She was beautiful and terrifying, just like Laima, and her sword was made of gold and studded with yellow gems. The other was pale, with straight black hair and east Asian features. Chinese, maybe. A silver suit that made her look like lightning. Two curved pieces of sharpened silver metal were propped against her throne. Unidentifiable, but clearly weapons.

If Laima was a goddess, the other two were likely goddesses as well. The other two fate goddesses that she'd mention?

Honestly, they all looked like freaking super heroes. And as much as they scared me, I wanted to *be* them.

I approached, trying to keep my knees steady. Though I was getting better with my new magic, if these ladies wanted to start a rumble, I'd end up on the bottom of the pile.

I stopped when I was about five meters away. Ares went to

stand off to the side, near Doyen and Magisteria, ready to bear witness but not participate. It was all me, whatever this was.

At the sight of Doyen and Magisteria, a scowl creased my face. I'd never like them, even if I became an ally.

I turned to the goddess. "I'm Phoenix Knight."

I had no idea what I was doing here, so I said no more.

"Phoenix Knight, I am Laima, one of the three fate goddesses." Her voice was deeper than it had been before, resonating with power. Since she was talking to me like she'd never met me, I just nodded.

The golden goddess spoke next. "I am Dekla, fate goddess."

I nodded, same as I had with Laima. I supposed I could bow, but it felt unnatural. And they weren't *my* goddesses.

The silver goddess went next. "And I am Karta. The completion of our trio."

I nodded, waiting expectantly for them to tell me what the hell was going on. The way their power filled the room kept me on my toes and ready to fight or flee, whichever seemed less deadly.

Karta rose, as graceful as water flowing down a bank. "This is the final stage of your journey. You have done well, Phoenix Knight."

"Thank you."

Dekla and Laima stood as well, their gazes riveted to me.

If this was the final stage of my journey, what the hell was going to happen? The three goddesses approached me, their power rolling off them. Unfortunately for me, their power had a hell of a kick. Crashing waves, thunder, and pure electricity were hell on a girl.

I stood as straight as I could. My knees shook, the tension in the air feeling like the only thing that kept me standing.

Each goddess neared, their faces terrible and beautiful. Sweat dripped down my temples.

"Can I ask what's happening?" I said.

"We will read your fate," Laima said. "As much as we can. To see what is relevant to the vampire realm."

Laima had told me some, but apparently there might be more. Perhaps they were more powerful as a trio?

I really didn't want to know my fate. A few hints, sure. But not too much detail. That'd just have me looking over my shoulder all the time.

But considering that I was currently surrounded by the three most powerful vampires and three badass goddesses, I didn't have much choice. Scratch that—*any* choice.

So I stood, as tall and straight as I could, while each goddess raised a hand and laid her fingertips upon my arms. Though the touch was light, their power zapped through me.

Three sets of eyes widened. The goddesses stared at me, shock clear on their faces. Laima's lips parted, a visual *holy shit* if I'd ever seen one.

What the hell had they seen? My heart raced a mile a minute.

Of all the challenges I'd faced, the goddesses were the worst. Their power buffeted me from all directions and they had clearly seen something bad. And all I could do was freaking stand there.

I'd rather fight my way out of something—but there was nothing to fight here. I'd just be an asshole who tried to shoot a goddess with her bow. And failed, of course.

I did *not* want to be that person.

As a unit, they stepped back, eyes still wide. They didn't look at each other, just turned and went back to their thrones. They sat, silent and still.

Every atom of my being screamed for information. As much as I hadn't wanted to know, I now silently screamed *Tell me what the hell is going on!*

Finally, Laima stood, her gaze heavy. She turned to Doyen and Magisteria. "You asked us to determine why she could walk in the Shadowlands. What makes her so special, and so dangerous, and if she can remain free without persecution for her species."

"Yes," Magisteria said.

"You can set aside the persecution idea right now," Laima said.

"What?" Doyen's voice was sharp.

"You heard me," Laima said. "Phoenix Knight is no normal FireSoul. She's going to save your asses one day. She's going to save all our asses."

Finally, I saw a hint of the Laima that I'd met earlier. But what the hell was she talking about?

"Phoenix Knight defies all your rules," Dekla said. "She is one of the Triumvirate, the three of power who are prophesied to save our world. Their tale is thousands of years old. We've been waiting for them. An apocalypse and a rejuvenation."

"That's a myth," Doyen said. "From the human world."

"Hardly," Karta said. "Two of the three members of the Triumvirate have completed their tasks. Phoenix's still remains, and I promise you—you want her to succeed. We *all* want her to succeed."

"Can you tell me anything about my role?" I asked. Laima hadn't told me much before, but maybe now…

"You represent Life in the Triumvirate," Dekla said. "Magic and Death have already come and gone, but Life remains."

"Your powers are related to that," Karta said. "Creation, destruction. It fits like the pieces of a puzzle. And you must embrace your magic."

"Even your new magic," Laima said. "A catalyst has occurred, your change has begun."

The same thing had happened to Del, who represented Death. Now it was my turn. The plant magic must be part of that.

"You will need help from your friends," Laima said.

Well, I could have told her that. Despite the dumb joke, I didn't feel like laughing.

"And help from the Vampire Court." Dekla's gaze cut toward

Ares, Doyen, and Magisteria.

Doyen and Magisteria looked gobsmacked, though Ares didn't look surprised a bit. Had he sensed something more in me? I liked the thought, but had no idea if it was true.

"You will regret it if you do not assist her." Laima's voice rang through the hall. "Not because we will seek vengeance. We will be as screwed as you are, if Nix does not succeed."

Holy fates. I was so not ready for that. From Cass and Del, I knew that the Triumvirate duties were important. But this?

This was hardcore.

And I really wanted some more details about the upcoming task. "Is there anything more that you can tell me about my task? I know that I must find the lost beaker, but beyond that, I have no idea."

"That is all we can see," Dekla said. "The rest is outside of the scope of our vision."

Damn. That left me in the dark. A lot of this information wasn't new to me, but having it confirmed by a seer speaking directly to me. And the idea that the Vampire Court must help me?

That was serious.

And my friends—

My comms charm ignited, Del's voice echoing out of the necklace. "Nix! Nix! Claire has been taken."

Suddenly, the room receded from my vision. "What?"

"They got her while we were on recon. We're going in tonight. We have to."

Shit. Shit. "Wait for me. I'm coming."

"Hurry."

The connection cut out. I looked up, gaze darting between the goddesses and the Vampire Court. Their magic still seethed in the room, overwhelming me with their power. I couldn't fight my way out of here, but if what the goddesses had said was true...

"I've got to go," I said.

Doyen stepped forward, her hand raised. "But—"

I pointed to the goddesses. "You heard them. You need me. And right now, I need to be back on earth, saving my friend. So I'm leaving." My gaze cut to Ares, and I couldn't help the plea in my eyes. As much as I was breaking out the badass boss lady persona, I still needed his help transporting out of here. "Get me out of here, will you?"

Ares nodded, striding toward me. Doyen and Magisteria stepped back, gazes resigned. Right before Ares reached me, I glanced at Laima. She winked, and just briefly, the goddess in the hot tub was back.

~

We arrived back at Factory Row moments later. It was late afternoon here, the sun just sinking toward the horizon. I pressed my fingertips to the comms charm. "Where are you guys?"

"P&P," Del said. "Come on. We need to recap."

I glanced at Ares. "Let's go."

I hurried down the street, Ares at my side. On the way toward P&P, I updated Ares on what we knew. "The man who killed Marin?" I said. "He—or his goons—just abducted my friend Claire."

"How?"

"We've been running recon on his compound outside of town." I glanced at him, seeing the shock on his face that I hadn't mentioned this. "I was going to tell you. I just wasn't sure how much I trusted you."

"Do you trust me now?" His gaze was serious as we walked.

"Yes. Enough to ask for your help in this."

"Why the recon?"

"The boss and his gang—we think it's a gang or something—stole an artifact from us. It was an ancient clay vase from the Bell Beaker Culture. Bronze Age."

"Why?" Shocked confusion laced Ares's voice, as if he couldn't imagine why someone would steal something like that.

"It's enchanted, like all the artifacts we recover. But we don't know what the spell is. Never could figure it out. That has to be why they took it, though."

"Sounds reasonable. How do you know it's the same people?"

"Most of them have the tattoo of a dragon. They got both the original artifact and the replica that I imbued with the magic. That alone is very weird—why not just go for the magic? That's all anyone wants from our artifacts, anyway."

"So we have to get that back and rescue your friend."

I nodded emphatically. "Yes."

We reached P&P and I pushed my way into the warmth of the cafe. There had been a *Closed* sign on the front, most likely because Connor wasn't about to serve scones and espresso while his sister was in the hands of a magical mob boss.

Everyone crowded around the bar, eying a piece of paper stretched out in front of them. Del, Roarke, Cass, Aidan, and Connor. They turned at the creaking sound of the door, looking at us.

"Thanks fates you're here," Del said.

Cass looked right at Ares. "Is she finally off the hook?"

"More than," he said. "And I'm here to help with Claire."

"Good. They've had her for two hours. We're going in as soon as it's dark." Cass pointed at the map. "Come check this out."

I approached the bar, eying the map. It was a plan of the dragon gang's compound, showing all the grounds and the factory.

"The exterior is accurate," Aidan said. "We were able to visually confirm that. The interior—that's more of a guess. It's the original builder's plan of the factory, but it's likely they modified things for their use."

"We've scouted the whole perimeter," Cass said. "Tested all the enchantments protecting the place. Even with Aidan's security breaking tricks, the only way to go in is by sea. There are fewer guards on that side. And no enchanted fences."

Ugh. The last thing I wanted was to get in another boat. But I nodded. "Any plans on how to do that?"

"A number," Connor said. "I've made enough invisibility potion for all of us. It'll last an hour. It won't protect us from everything—there are enchantments that could reveal us—but it should help a lot."

"And Roarke has gotten us a boat," Cass said. "I can use my illusion power to make it blend in with the sea."

"And I can use my ability to muffle sound to quiet the engine," Del said. "We should at least be able to get onto the beach without them detecting us. From there, we find Claire and the beaker."

"Oh, man. That's a lot of unknowns." I grinned. "But then, we're used to that."

"Aren't we ever." Cass looked up at the clock. "Two hours until dark. We don't want to approach until then. The dark will make it easier for me to conceal the boat. But we can get going in ten minutes. The boat is in the port, which is about a one-hour ride from the compound."

"Yeah, we should be ready to make a move as soon as possible." Unfortunately, my magic felt drained and I was exhausted, but I'd find some energy somewhere.

I had to.

Everyone left the coffeeshop to gather whatever they needed for the assault on the compound. I was about to head to my apartment for a quick change of clothes when Ares touched my arm.

"Wait," he said.

I stopped, turning to him. Connor had gone into the back, no doubt to pack his potion bombs for the attack, and we were alone in the shop.

"How are you?" Concern laced his voice. "The goddesses... that was heavy stuff."

"I'm good." I had a *lot* to think about. But I couldn't think about it now.

"You're more than good. You were amazing," he said. "You won every challenge, never sacrificing what was important. You awed me."

"Wow." Heat warmed my cheeks. "Thanks."

"And the Vampire Court is now on your side. It's done."

"I thought I'd have to meet with Magisteria and Doyen again? Make it official?"

His gaze darkened. "I'll deal with them. The fates made it clear —*you* made it clear—how important you are to all of us. We're in your debt."

"So it's officially over."

"It is." He stepped closer, towering over me. Heat filled his gaze. He reached out, cupping the back of my neck.

I gasped at the gentle touch of his strong hand, fire igniting in my belly. His scent wrapped around me, rich and lovely and *him.*

"I'm going to kiss you now." His words had days of pent-up desire in them, as if he'd been holding onto them since the trials began.

He'd given me my chance to step back, to say no. No way was I going to do it. We only had a few moments, if that. But I'd take them. I'd take whatever I could get, as crazy as it was.

My breath caught in my throat at the hot look in Ares's eyes. He crushed his lips to mine. Heat streaked across my skin and I sunk my hands into his hair, holding tight as his lips plundered my own. He groaned low in his throat, an animal sound that made me shiver.

I swiped my tongue across his, desperate for one taste, then pulled away.

He stepped back, drew in a ragged breath. "Let's go save your friend."

CHAPTER TWELVE

Ten minutes later, after running up to my apartment for a change of clothes and a granola bar, I rode in the back of Cass's car. She and Del sat up front. I'd insisted that Ares go with Roarke, Aidan, and Connor because I'd wanted a moment to talk to my *deirfiúr*.

And frankly, he was a distraction.

"How'd it go in the Vampire Court trials?" Del asked.

"Crazy." I shook my head, remembering. "They've got some weird magical creatures there. But it was the goddesses who were the weirdest."

"Goddesses?" Cass asked.

"Yeah." I described Laima, Karta, and Dekla to them, along with what they had said about me and my power.

"Wow," Cass said. "But then, we've always known that you're special."

"That we're all special," I said. "But didn't that sound pretty...intense?"

"It sounds world saving," Del said. "Which isn't a huge surprise given that you are Life in the Triumvirate."

"Yeah, without you, there's nothing." Cass turned sharply onto the road leading to the port. "Zip, nada, nothing."

"It's a lot of pressure." I did *not* want to fail at this.

"Fortunately, you're used to pressure," Del said. "These last few months haven't been easy. Hell, our life hasn't. But we're doing fine."

"As long as we get Claire back." My stomach turned. The idea of something happening to Claire...our best friend...

I couldn't bear to think of it. She was tough. She was a damned mercenary, for fate's sake. She could handle herself until we got there.

"We'll get her back," Del said. "And we'll take care of this dragon gang too."

"I'm really starting to hate those bastards." My fists clenched.

Cass pulled the car to a stop at the port. Though Magic's Bend was near the sea, it was just far enough away that we didn't have much of a touristy developed seaside. Mostly just a port for receiving shipments and some fishing boats.

There were several large docks and a number of smaller ones for pleasure boats and the fishing craft.

It was busy at this hour, everyone bustling around, finishing up for the day. The guys had already arrived and stood at the head of one of the smaller docks, waiting for us.

We joined them, weaving around a man in a forklift who was delivering crates of fruit to a waiting truck.

For these folks, everything was just so *normal*. For us... our friend's life hung in the balance. It was everything. I wanted everyone else to be as freaked out as I was, but that was obviously a shit plan.

So I fixed my gaze on Roarke and tried to focus on the business at hand. "Is the boat ready?"

"Should be," he said. "Belongs to a demon employee of mine."

We followed him down the dock, which bobbed underfoot. The water was dark and still, with bits of seaweed floating on top. The boat was docked at the end, a big white powerboat that looked fast.

Good. Fast was exactly what we wanted.

A demon waited beside it, his small horns poking out of his dark hair. Otherwise, he looked human, which didn't necessarily mean that he was a good guy. But if he was with Roarke, Warden of the Underworld, then he was probably fine. Not all demons were evil—though most were—and those that weren't had an opportunity to live on earth if they worked for Roarke and followed the rules.

"Hey boss." The demon nodded at Roarke. "Ready to go?"

"Yes. Thanks, Quincy. We'll take good care of it."

Quincy nodded, his gaze uneasy, as if he were worried we'd wreck the thing. But I guessed you didn't say no to the Warden of the Underworld when he asked you for a favor.

We climbed on board, the seven of us barely fitting in the cockpit. Quincy undid the lines and tossed them into the boat. Roarke, apparently some kind of boater himself, turned on the engine and pulled the boat away from the dock.

The wind was cold out in the harbor. I shivered and zipped up my jacket.

Connor handed out the invisibility potions, saying, "I'll give the signal to drink."

Cass turned to the group, shouting over the wind. "If we get separated, I don't know if we can transport out of the compound. We're not sure about the extent of the protection charms. So get back to the boat—it's out best way out."

I swallowed hard. Great. That could get sticky.

The waves got bigger as Roarke steered the boat out of the harbor and into the Pacific. As soon as we were out of the low-wake zone, he cranked the throttle and we took off. I grabbed a hand rail and braced myself against the bouncing of the waves. Wind whipped at my hair, cold stinging my cheeks.

I had no idea what we were going into, or what was coming after we finished this. If we finished it. The goddesses of fate had said some crazy things. It was just so hard to imagine that *I* would be the one to save us all. Or whatever.

It was almost too big for my mind to comprehend.

I might have known this was coming—my role in the Triumvirate had been revealed months ago—but the extent of it? That was a shock.

The sun set behind the horizon about thirty minutes into our journey, leaving us with a warm pink sky and an ocean that glinted with pale orange.

About twenty minutes later, Connor shouted to the group, "Drink your potions."

I dug the little vial out of my pocket and met Ares's gaze. "Enjoy. They're tasty."

I slugged mine down, grimacing at the muddy taste that I'd learned to despise. Across from me, Ares grimaced.

"Liar," he muttered.

I laughed as the potion's shivery chill worked its way through me. Because we'd all taken the same batch, we'd be able to see each other.

Next to me, Del gripped a hand rail and closed her eyes. Her magic swelled on the air, the scent of fresh soap strange with the scent of the sea air.

A moment later, the sound of the engine cut abruptly. It was almost as if Roarke had cranked it off. But we kept powering across the waves, fast as ever.

Cass cracked her knuckles and smiled at me. "Time to practice."

Because of her role in the Triumvirate, Cass had a massive amount of magical power. She represented Magic, after all. She also had a number of magical gifts to call from. Not all were easy to manipulate, and illusion had always been one of the tougher ones for her.

I held my breath as her magic shimmered on the air, rolling

across my skin and into the boat. Slowly, the boat began to turn transparent until it finally disappeared.

Below my feet, I saw nothing but the water, waves crushed by the weight of the boat passing over them. My stomach dropped at the strange sight. "Wicked."

"Those are some serious talents, Cass and Del," Ares said.

"We're the ultimate stealth team," Cass said. "I can't do too much more with this magic—it's too difficult to control—but hopefully I can hold it till we reach the compound."

"Speaking of." I pointed to the massive building on the beach, just a couple miles away. All of the lights in the windows were dimmed, as if some kind of concealment charm had been placed on the windows.

"They're committed to keeping a low profile," Aidan muttered. "That kind of magic is expensive."

Roarke slowed the boat as we approached the shore. We were about two hundred meters away when the boat stopped abruptly, as if it had been grabbed by a giant hand.

"What the hell?" Roarke jiggled the throttle, but the boat didn't move.

"Protective barrier," Aidan said.

"We can break through—"

A massive jolt cut off Ares's words. The boat bounced on the water, then was pulled underneath the surface. It was as if a hand had reached up and pulled the boat into the depths, and it happened in an instant. One second, I was standing on the deck, the next, I was thrashing in the water with my friends.

The cold drove the air from my lungs as the seaweed wrapped around my legs, yanking me under. Shock made me open my mouth to scream, but instead of making a sound, I gulped in water. Frantic, I struggled to break free, opening my eyes.

At first it was dark, then light blared from my left. It was Ares, doing his hand light trick. The one where he shined the glow out of his palm. It illuminate

witnessed.

All of my friends were

surface of the water. The

thighs and arms as they st

strong enough and fast en

kelp, but more kept com

pulling him deeper.

Cass and Aidan transfor

kelp's grip with their great

could do was thrash. The co

tioning themselves belo

them hard enough to

swim to the surface

Ares and Ro

I kicked

Freaki

I

yo

There was no fighting such a strange enemy.

My lungs ached and my heartbeat thundered in my ears, deafening.

Beneath us, the boat was tangled in a huge mass of weeds. Cass must have lost control of her illusion magic.

The kelp had attacked us, dragging the whole boat down!

The boat below us was strangled by weeds, looking a hell of a lot like the Pūķi trapped by the acid vines.

I didn't hesitate, just prayed to the fates that my magic worked on sea plants. And that I had enough of it to go around.

With everything I had, I pushed my magic into the kelp around us, trying to form the same connection I'd had with the acid vines.

Do my bidding. Release us.

At first, nothing happened. It didn't even feel like my magic entered the weeds. So I pushed harder, gripping the seaweed around my waist and trying to imagine that we were one. That my will was its will.

After a moment, the kelp loosened. I thrashed, struggling for the surface. But I was so weak, my muscles seizing from the cold and my lungs burning.

Cass and Aidan were the first to break free of the loosened kelp. They sped toward Connor and Del, who were closest, posi-

the struggling people and pushing
break the bonds of the kelp so they could

arke broke free on their own, racing for air.
and thrashed, but I was slow.
ng seaweed.
commanded it to push me toward the surface. *Help me! Do
ur flipping job, kelp!*

The plants were mine to command. I knew it. So I'd make it happen. I *had* to make it happen.

I pushed my will into the kelp, forcing it to gather under me like a raft and push me toward the surface. It worked, shooting me through the water like a cannon. I burst to the surface, coughing and sucking in air.

All around me, my friends treaded water under the moonlight. Four humans and two sea lions.

"Well that went to shit," Del whispered.

I choked a low laugh, aware that voices could travel well over the sea. There weren't supposed to be a lot of guards watching the shore, but I didn't want to alert any of them to our presence.

"We'd better swim for it," Ares said.

"Just two hundred yards." It looked like forever, but we'd manage.

We set out, cutting across the water as waves buffeted us. The water was freezing, making my teeth chatter and my fingers numb. In the chill, my strokes were weak and awkward, but I gave it my all, muscles straining and lungs burning. I still hadn't caught my breath yet, but there was no stopping this. We needed to get to land.

Beside me, Ares swam like he was a freaking Olympian. *Vampires.*

Roarke had shifted into his demon form, bursting out of the water and taking to the sky with his wings. He picked up Del and carried her along. A sea lion—I assumed it was Cass—joined me and I grabbed on, holding her loosely about the neck. The other sea lion helped Connor, who wasn't faring much better than I.

We could swim, but two hundred meters across open ocean in the north Pacific was not a great way to start our assault on a magically reinforced compound owned by supernatural gangsters.

We reached land and crawled out onto the shore, gasping. Ares walked out of the sea like a freaking merman with legs, as if swimming through the icy Pacific for two hundred meters was nothing. Aidan and Cass transformed back to their human selves.

"Thanks," I gasped, shaking from the cold. "The ride was great."

Roarke landed next to us, setting Del on the ground.

We were all accounted for and standing, thank fates.

"Let's get a move on," Connor said. "Only forty minutes left on this invisibility potion."

We turned toward the old factory, which sat a few hundred yards back, high on a hill. Tiny black shapes were moving toward us, racing across the grass.

"Shit. Dogs." Twelve of them, at least.

I broke into a run, sprinting for the left side of the house, where there were less of the animals. My wet clothes were horribly uncomfortable, but at least the exertion warmed me up.

My friends followed, racing alongside. The guard dogs were quick, wheeling to chase us. Though we were invisible, they could smell us, no question. As they neared, I realized they were some hybrid form of wolf and dog, their fangs gleaming white in the moonlight.

Or were they hellhounds?

I could shoot them with arrows or my friends could blast them with magic, but I hated the idea of killing them, and I knew Cass and Del would be with me. Demons were one thing. Animals another.

It's not like these were bad dogs—they just had bad owners

who trained them to bite people instead of squeaky toys. I wasn't going to blame the dog, even though I *really* didn't want to become a squeaky toy.

And the commotion would probably get us caught, anyway.

Connor dug into the satchel at his waist, pulling out several small glass spheres filled with potion. He handed them off to me and Ares.

"Sleeping potion." He panted.

"Thanks." A dog got close enough that my odds were good, so I took aim and fired. The blue globe flew through the air, exploding against the hound's side in a flash of blue. The beast gave a few more awkward steps, then collapsed against the grass, dead asleep.

"How many of those do you have?" Del asked.

"Only six." Connor hurled one at another dog, who passed out immediately.

There were at least twelve dogs.

"Pond Flower!" Del called softly. I could barely hear her over my pounding heart.

A moment later, a white and brown dog appeared at Del's side. Pond Flower was a hellhound who had adopted Del a couple of months ago. Despite her name—which she'd given herself—Pond Flower was a hellhound. She was like Del's familiar, almost.

"Friends." Del pointed at the other dogs. "Make friends."

Make them *our* friends, I could hear her saying.

Pond Flower grinned, her pink tongue lolling out of her mouth, and spun around to charge the dogs. She gave a low, happy woof, running in circles around the other dogs.

They stilled in their tracks, staring at her.

I kept running, praying it would work. Del could communicate with Pond Flower and she, hopefully, could communicate with the others.

Since we only had a few non-lethal weapons, it was our only chance to get out of here without bloodshed or being caught.

"I think it's working," Del gasped from beside me.

I turned my head, craning my neck to get a peek. Pond Flower was holding off the other dogs, her fur blazing with her protective black flame. She only broke that out occasionally, and I hoped she was doing it now to prove that she was the Alpha.

At least the dogs weren't chasing us any longer, so I figured it was working.

We were still forty meters from the building when one of the back doors opened and figures spilled out onto the grass.

Guards. Demons, from the look of their horns. They couldn't see us—not as long as this invisibility potion held out—but they had to be wondering what the hell the guard dogs were up to.

"Go!" I hissed. "To the bushes!"

My friends sprinted toward cover as I conjured my bow and dropped to my knee, taking aim. The first arrow pierced a demon in the neck, the second went straight through another demon's eye. *Gag.*

I took out the last four in quick succession.

Ares ran straight for the demons, fast as lightning. He grabbed two by the legs and dragged them into the bushes, returning for the other four. Within moments, the scene had been cleared as if they'd never come outside.

I sure hoped they were the only ones who'd wondered about the dogs' activity. I gripped my bow and ran for my friends, joining them in the shadows of the large hedges.

Pond Flower sat in the yard with the guard dogs, keeping them at bay. They were either her friends or her minions, but it didn't really matter as long as they left us alone.

The others turned to face me.

Cass whispered, "Ready?"

CHAPTER THIRTEEN

"Ready," I whispered.

I called upon my dragon sense, just like we'd planned. Cass and Del did the same, all of us searching for Claire. She was the priority, then the beaker, then information about the dragon gang.

"I've got something," Cass said.

I got a tug too, directing me into the building. "Me too."

"Subtly first," I said. "Don't let them know we're here."

Though we had enough magical firepower to light this place up, that defied the point of safely rescuing Claire and recovering a delicate artifact.

Stealth was our best bet, here.

As a group, we crept toward the double doors that our demon attackers had spilled from. One by one, we slipped into a massive foyer. The floor was marble and the chandelier pure gold. My FireSoul tugged toward it, confirming its nature.

It looked like it should be in a mansion instead of an old factory—the mob boss had done some decorating, it seemed.

"Swanky place," Cass whispered.

"No kidding. Someone is establishing their status." At least the foyer was empty. Whoever had been in here had run out to see what the dogs were up to, but apparently hadn't alerted anyone else. Thank fates for small favors.

We crept through the foyer and down a wide hallway paneled in gold silk. Crystal chandeliers dotted the hallway, sending sparkling light over the gleaming wood floor.

Whoever lived here wanted everyone to know that he was doing *well*. It had to cost a hell of a lot to do up an old factory like this. But then, money wasn't a problem for this guy, it seemed. And he'd want to maintain a low-profile, so using this old place was ideal.

We took several turns, winding our way through the labyrinthine structure and passing by several groups of guards in various rooms. Some played poker in a library, others ate pizza in a small kitchen. They all looked like bruisers and most sported visible dragon tattoos.

This place was like a mobster's hangout, where they killed time between crimes and whatever other crap mobsters did. Most of the groups perked up when we snuck by. Even though they seemed to sense a change in the energy, they didn't see us.

We reached a wide hall that was less glamorously decorated. At the end, two hulking guards stood in front of a door. They were demons, their large horns protruding from their heads. Weapons hung off their vests, gleaming in the light.

My dragon sense pulled hard toward the door they guarded.

I pointed, nodding. Cass and Del nodded as well, their dragon senses backing me up.

"Who's there?" The guard's voice was gruff, suspicious.

"Show yourself!" demanded the other.

Connor stepped forward, hurling one of his sleeping potions right at the guard on the left. It exploded against his chest in a splash of blue, and he keeled over.

The other guard began to shout, but I fired an arrow directly into his neck. He gurgled and fell.

With the guards out, we ran toward the door. It was a massive wooden affair, with a heavy padlock near the handle. Unfortunately, it wasn't a normal lock, with a keyhole that I could pick. This one was magical.

Aidan, our resident magical security expert, reached for it, his fingers outstretched warily. He touched the metal briefly, then withdrew his hand. "Enchanted."

Shit.

He dug into his pocket and pulled out a spell stripper, a rare artifact that my *deirfiúr* and I had envied as soon as we'd realized he had one. It allowed him to break past almost any enchantment, which would come in handy in our work.

Aidan ran the little silver orb around the lock, then frowned. "It's not working."

"That's rare," Cass said.

"So are the enchantments protecting the compound," he said.

"We'll have to break the door down," Ares said.

"Too loud." My mind raced. "We're trapped back here. I don't want demons catching us."

"Any ideas, then?" Del asked.

"Yeah." I sucked in a breath and touched my fingertips to the metal lock. The magic within the metal pricked against my skin, stinging like little wasp attacks. I closed my mind against the pain, focusing on my Destroyer magic. Envisioning it as a wind that I forced into the lock.

Break. Crumble. Disappear.

It took a moment as my magic swirled inside of me, but eventually the lock began to crumble away.

"Wicked!" Connor said.

"New talent," I murmured.

The last of the metal fell away. I pushed against the door. It swung open to reveal a dark, windowless room. Claire sat propped against the wall, her head slumped over her shoulder. I rushed in, my friends following.

Before I reached her, a commotion sounded from behind us. I glanced back, catching sight of demons flooding into the hall down the way. Six of them at least.

Immediately, two of them hurled blue balls of magic that I'd never seen before. They coalesced in the air to form rocks, one of which glanced right off of Connor's head. He collapsed against the ground, a rag doll.

"I've got this," Ares said. He sprinted down the hall toward the demons, dodging their blasts of magic and colliding with the first two like a tornado.

He was so fast, and so strong, that he'd broken three necks within the first three seconds. Working in such close proximity, boxed in by all the walls, gave him a massive advantage. The enemy had nowhere to run, except back the way they had come, and he took out the demons in record time.

I turned back to Claire, dropping to my knees beside her.

Her dark hair fell into her eyes and a nasty bruise bloomed on her cheek. Del and Cass crowded around me.

Aidan and Roarke were tending to Connor.

Gently, I shook Claire's shoulder. "Come on, wake up, pal."

Groggily, she shook her head. When her gaze landed on us, her eyes brightened. "Knew you guys would make it."

Her words were slightly slurred, and I realized her lips were fatter than normal. Whatever had happened, Claire had put up a fight. And since she was such a badass, whoever she'd been fighting had been no slouch.

Anger seethed in my chest, a black tar of rage that threatened to consume me.

"Are you okay?" I asked.

"Fine." She struggled to stand. We helped her.

On the ground, Connor was still out cold.

"We've got to get them out of here," I said.

"Aidan and Roarke can fly them out, over the sea," Cass said. "We'll go get the beaker. And the bastard who did this."

I nodded. It was the best plan. Claire could ride Aidan in his griffon form, and Roarke, who hadn't transformed from his demon shape, could carry the unconscious Connor.

I hugged Claire, who returned the gesture, though weakly. "I'm sorry you got nabbed."

"Eh, no problem." She pulled back and smiled. "Now go get those bastards."

I grinned—which was really more a baring of my non-existent fangs—and nodded. Aidan helped Claire down the hall while Roarke carried an unconscious Connor. Cass, Del, Ares, and I split off from them, intent on finding the boss and the beaker.

My dragon sense pulled me back the way we came, so we snuck back by several of the rooms full of gangsters. We were lucky that they hadn't heard the commotion, but tension tightened my skin anyway as we crept past the open doors full of criminals.

I imagined that any one of them could have beaten up Claire, and though I wanted to go in there and crack some heads, we really needed to find the boss.

We'd just crept by the last open door when my skin pricked coldly.

Shit.

"Invisibility charm is wearing off," I whispered. We'd used up our whole hour.

But we were close to our destination. I could feel it. Just up one floor. When we reached a massive foyer with a grand staircase, it was clear which way we should go. As a group, we hovered in the doorway, checking out the foyer and stairs for any threats.

"Clear," Ares whispered. "I hear nothing."

His hearing was better than ours, so I'd take him at his word. We hurried across the gleaming marble floor and up the thick dark carpet covering the stairs. I followed my dragon sense left, heading down a wide hall that was a good fifty feet long.

This place was enormous.

We were about halfway down the hall and almost to our destination by the time the horde of demons appeared. Ten, total. There were some mages too, from the look of them, and all looked shocked, then pissed as hell to see us.

Two mages raised their hands, a surefire signal that they were about to throw some kind of magic at us.

Shit.

My heart thundered. Quickly, I conjured a barrier of sandbags, which were surprisingly good at blocking magic and fireballs. As a unit, Cass, Del, and I dropped to our knees behind the barrier.

Ares, marching to the beat of his own drummer, leapt over the thing right as a demon threw a fireball at us. The vampire dodged it, racing toward the attackers.

"Keep to the left!" I called as I fired an arrow down the right side of the hall. It pierced a demon right through the neck and he tumbled backward.

Cass and Del threw fireballs and icicles, keeping their attack to the right side of the hall so they wouldn't hit Ares. But the precaution was unnecessary. He was so fast that he took out three demons, all while avoiding our blasts. It was like he could keep track of the demons and our weapons simultaneously, delivering death blows while dodging Cass's fireballs, Del's icicles, and my arrows.

All the while, our attackers hurled fireballs and great blasts of wind at our sandbag barrier. One of the wind blasts hit me in the face, throwing me backward. I crashed against the ground, pain flaring in my back.

I blinked, clearing my vision, then scrambled upward as Cass was blasted backward by another shot of wind. Fortunately, Del nailed the elemental mage right in the chest. Her icicle plunged gruesomely into muscle and flesh, sending the mage hurtling backward.

Ares broke the neck of the last demon, and the hall grew quiet.

"Come on!" I leapt over the sandbag barrier. The commotion we'd caused had *definitely* alerted anyone else in the building.

We raced down the hall toward the door at the end. It was closed, but my dragon sense was dead certain it was our destination.

And stealth was no longer an option.

"Break down the door," I said to Ares, knowing he could take it out in a flash.

Ares sprinted ahead, crashing through the wooden door like a freaking cannon. We followed, racing into the room.

The scene was so cliched I almost laughed. I would have, if the cold, dark magic floating in the room hadn't made me want to wet my pants.

It vibrated from the man sitting at the wide, wooden desk.

The Master, as Aleric had called him.

No question about it.

Time slowed in my head as I took in the surroundings. It wasn't just my fright or the stress. No—this man was part of my fate. *This* was my fate, a snowball that was about to roll down a mountain, gaining size and momentum with every inch until it exploded against a tree or some other immoveable force.

This was the moment the snowball went over the edge of the mountain.

The man at the desk was pale with dark hair, wearing a fancy suit and half a dozen golden rings on his frighteningly elegant fingers. His eyes were black pits, like there was no soul within. Just a direct access portal to hell. The magic that rolled off him smelled like rotting garbage and felt like a kick to the gut.

Two beakers sat in front of him, identical clay vases.

My beakers.

Around him, massive men in suits shoved papers and objects into heavy black briefcases.

182

"Making a run for it?" I asked.

My friends didn't wait for the answer. They immediately began to hurl fireballs and icicles at the man behind the desk. He raised a hand, creating a forcefield that deflected the weapons.

"You've compromised our location." His voice was so cold that I shivered.

His shield began to crack a moment later, a white line streaking down through the invisible forcefield. He looked at the men to his right, gaze calm. "Attack."

I drew my bow, firing an arrow at the man nearest Del. It pierced him in the neck. Ares moved like lighting, his shadow sword drawn and his face a deadly mask. He took down the boss's minions left and right, but more flowed into the room.

Cass's next fireball put a huge shatter mark on the boss's invisible shield. His brow furrowed.

He reached for the beaker. Del shot an icicle. It crashed against the shield, plowing through it and slicing across the boss's arm. Blood spurted.

He cursed and grabbed the briefcase nearest him, then reached below the desk for a moment. He didn't pull anything out, but turned and ran, straight for a door behind his desk.

He left the beakers, which apparently weren't worth *that* much to him.

I sprinted after him. "I've got him!"

"We're coming!" Cass yelled. One of her fireballs exploded against the wall to my right.

She, Del, and Ares were still busy fighting off the boss's goons as I chased him through the doorway and up a narrow set of stairs. They curved around and I lost sight of him, but I could hear his pounding footsteps.

We climbed at least two stories up, but he was always just out of sight. Above, a door slammed open and a loud roar filled the stairwell. I sprinted harder, pushing myself as my lungs burned and my heart thundered.

I couldn't lose him.

I spilled out onto the rooftop. A helicopter was waiting for the man. The rotors spun, blasting wind that tore at my hair and made my eyes water.

The boss was sprinting toward the open chopper door, his stride sure and quick. He wore a suit but ran like a warrior.

I raised my bow and fired, right for his back. The shot was true, the arrow flying straight.

The chopper pilot flung out his hand, sending a streak of lighting right for my arrow. It collided with the slender shaft, incinerating it in an instant.

A moment later, he threw another bolt at me. I dived to the side, crashing against the cement roof and barely avoiding the lighting.

I scrambled up just as the boss jumped into the helicopter. It took off immediately, flying high into the sky. I stood, rage and panic fighting within me. My mind raced, searching for a way—any way—to stop them.

Wind from the sea whipped over the roof as my comms charm vibrated with magic.

"Get off the roof!" Cass screamed. "Bomb! Six seconds!"

Holy shit!

My skin chilled as instinct took over. Instantly, I realized what he'd done when he'd reached under the desk. He'd pressed the button for a bomb, destroying all evidence that this place might contain. Just like his men ate the cyanide tablets so that we couldn't learn from their bodies.

I dropped my bow and sprinted for the side of the roof, mind suddenly cold and calculating. Five seconds left. I was four stories up. Too far to jump, too short a time to rappel down.

That left only one option.

Flight.

In a huge surge, I pushed all my magic toward my conjuring gift, creating a small hang glider. It took all of my magic to conjure it the way it needed to be—with the harness already around my waist. Four seconds left.

My hands gripped the bars and the harness wrapped around my waist as I sprinted full tilt for the edge of the roof. Three seconds left.

I leapt off the edge, praying as the hang glider caught the strong sea wind and carried me away from the building. Two stories below me, a huge glass window shattered, the glass flying outward. A griffon charged out into the night sky, Del clinging to her back. Ares leapt from the window, landing on the lawn with a feral grace. He sprinted away as the griffon flew high into the sky.

The blast rocked my world, deafening me. The force of the blow tore the fabric from my hang glider. Heat warmed me, fiery hot. I tumbled, end over end, as the explosion pushed me away from the building.

I was still two stories above the ground, going way too fast and way too out of control. Beneath me, Ares sprinted as if to catch me.

Insane man!

The broken hang glider flapped around me as I tumbled through the air. I neared the ground, Ares racing closer. Just as I was about to plow into the lawn, he lunged for me, snagging me out of the air.

His superior speed kept us moving for only a fraction of a second. Then we were tumbling in a tangle of limbs, the plastic posts of the hang glider tearing away as our bodies battered the ground.

We skidded to a stop, dirt and grass flying up around us.

Every inch of my body hurt. My head spun, my vision was nearly blacked out. I groaned, rolling over.

"You okay?" Ares grunted, slowly sitting up.

"Yeah." My ribs sang with pain—definitely broken—and my arm hung at a funny angle. Blood dripped into my right eye, but I only needed one to see the inferno that was the building. "Holy shit."

It was a massive fireball, so big that it lit up the lawn like it was daytime. Cass and Del were on the ground about fifty yards to our left, not looking much better than us. The blast must have blown them out of the sky too. Cass, still in griffon form, got unsteadily to her legs. Del struggled to stand as well.

Pond Flower, along with the rest of the dogs, sprinted toward them. At least they hadn't been in the building when the blast had gone off.

Roarke, Aidan, Connor, and Claire were nowhere to be seen, but they'd had enough time to escape. Though fear for them simmered in my chest, I suppressed it. They would be okay. They *had* to be okay.

I looked at Ares, my head spinning. "You caught me."

He grimaced. "That's a bit generous."

True. It was more like he'd gotten in my way and partially slowed my hurtling trajectory towards death. But it'd kept me alive.

"Thanks," I said. "My hang glider idea was pretty insane. My odds weren't great."

"I thought it was genius." Ares grinned, his smile painful. I'd bet he had some broken bones, too. "You're a badass, Nix."

I grinned. Though my whole body ached from an unknown number of injuries, his words warmed me.

I reached out and grabbed him by the back of the neck, pulling his face towards mine. I planted a hard kiss on his lips, tasting blood and sweat from our near escape. Warmth filled me, healing and good.

We'd made it out. We'd all made it out.

And I was going to be grateful for that. We'd survived.

CHAPTER FOURTEEN

As it turned out, I'd barely survived. The fall had broken more bones than I'd realized and caused some internal bleeding that the healers had just barely managed to stop in time.

Apparently adrenaline had made me able to sit up after the explosion. After Cass, Del, and Pond Flower had reached us, I'd passed right out.

Or so they'd told me. I'd woken up in the hospital the next day. Ares's blood donation had helped, but I'd needed a few nights in the hospital to sort everything out. I wasn't sure how I felt about having more of his blood, but since I'd have died otherwise, I couldn't complain too much.

Everyone had been in bad shape, but we were now on the mend. Some magic and R&R had my bones mended and my cuts healed. I felt like I'd been run over by a small car rather than a bus, which was a win. An hour ago, Del and Cass had picked me up at the hospital. We were now settled in at my apartment.

I was propped up in the corner of the couch, a plate of cheese pizza and Cass and Del on the cushions next to me.

A knock sounded at the door.

"Come in!" I called.

Claire opened the door and stepped in, followed by Connor. Her bruises had faded and Connor now wore only a bandaid on his head.

"You look good!" Claire said.

I grinned. "Thanks! I feel only slightly like crap. Which is a remarkable improvement."

"I can't believe you jumped off the roof in a hang glider," Connor said.

"Yeah, that was nuts." I still couldn't believe I'd done that. Not like I'd had many options, but that had just been crazy. These last few days had been as nuts as a squirrel's refrigerator. "You look a lot better, too, Claire."

She smiled. "Thanks. I feel a lot better. Thanks for getting me out of there."

"Duh," Cass, Del, and I said in unison.

"Just sorry you got nabbed." Cass turned to me. "We were trying to find a weak spot in the fence's enchantments when the goons came out. Overpowered us."

"He did have a lot of back-up. Dozens of men," I said.

"That he blew up." Del shook her head, clearly horrified. "He just fried them all."

"Monster," Claire said.

"But it means he probably has a lot more men where those came from," I said. Another knock sounded at the door. "Come in!"

Ares, Roarke, and Aidan stepped in. Ares's gaze went immediately to me. He hadn't left my side at the hospital, according to Del, though he'd bailed as soon as I'd woken. To deal with something at the Vampire Court, he'd said.

"How are you feeling, Nix?" Roarke asked.

"A lot better." I pointed to the kitchen. "There's drinks. Help yourself."

I sipped my well-deserved glass of Four Roses on the rocks, sighing contentedly at the burn. On the coffee table sat the two beakers that the mob boss had stolen. Ares had managed to grab them before jumping out of the window. Back at the compound, he had set them on the grass before catching me, which had been quick thinking, because otherwise they'd have ended up as shattered as my bones and then we'd have lost the magic for good.

Everyone grabbed drinks from the kitchen and then piled into the living room.

"So, who wants to start?" I said. We needed a recap of what had happened, and each of us had different pieces of the puzzle.

Claire raised her hand. "Me."

"Perfect." I sipped my drink. "What'd you learn while those jerks were beating the crap out of you?"

"Dicks," Del muttered.

"Rotten weasel shits," Cass added.

Ares's brows rose, but he just grinned.

"I didn't hear much," Claire said. "But I did learn that he's some kind of crime lord who has been in operation for decades."

"He looked younger than that." I recalled his smooth skin and dark hair. "Forties, maybe."

"Might be a long-lived species," Cass said.

"No one said what he was," Claire said. "But he's working on some goal he's obsessed with. He's got strongholds all over the world. Asia and Europe were the two I heard of, but don't know where."

That matched with what Ares had learned, so that was good.

"And Magic's Bend?" Ares asked.

"This one is new," she said. "The guards were saying how much they preferred this place to the ones in Asia and Europe— that's how I figured that out."

"Makes sense," Aidan says. "They kept a low profile by quietly renovating an abandoned factory that's been on the outskirts for years, but they couldn't have been here for more than a couple months without the Order of the Magica figuring something was up."

"So he's moving into new territory," I said. "Or at least, he was."

"Yeah. Whatever his end goal is, it was worth blowing up his fancy compound to protect."

"Did you learn anything about dragons?" Cass asked. "Or what they want with them?"

Claire shook her head. "Since dragons are long dead, I don't know what they're planning to try to get. I know you said there was a prophecy with the word dragon and return in it, so it's got to be that."

I nodded. "Agreed. But what...I have no idea."

Del leaned forward and picked up one of the beakers. It was the original—I could always tell my replicas from the originals. She handed it to me. I took it, the clay rough against my fingertips. Magic surged through my hands.

I glanced up at everyone, surprised. "They've transferred the magic back to the original."

"Why?" Ares asked.

"I don't know." I stared hard at it. "Must have been important for some reason."

"They said something about drinking from it," Claire said. "That the bossman drank from some weird old jug. That must be it."

"Huh." I inspected the beaker, feeling the magic that had been indecipherable. It was rare I couldn't identify the magic in an artifact. "Perhaps that's what this thing does. It makes a potion or something. That's where the magic is."

"Which means that if the boss drank from it, he's gotten its power," Ares said.

"Or something." I frowned, worry a heavy weight in my belly. "The boss reached for it before he left. Which means it has more use in it. But he wasn't desperate to have it, because he ditched once it got risky. So he got whatever he really needed from it."

"And it probably has to do with dragons," Cass said. "Right?"

"Right." Del nodded. "They've got dragon tattoos and the prophecy Nix learned says dragons."

"But what the hell does it all mean?" I asked. We had threads—several of them. But they were all loose and totally confusing.

"I don't know," Ares said. "But we'll figure this out. The Vampire Court is also invested in this."

"Because the boss killed your friend Marin," Cass said.

"Yes. But also because it's important to Nix. We're bound to support her in this." His tone was heavy. Deadly serious.

"Because of what the fate goddesses said?" I asked.

"Yes. And because even without them saying you're important, it's obvious. Whatever is going on, we need to get to the bottom of it. An immensely powerful supernatural—one who stunk of evil—is sacrificing millions of dollars to accomplish this goal. That goal can't be good. He can't be allowed to achieve it."

I nodded, agreeing wholeheartedly. The fact that the boss had blown up his whole compound—with all the men inside—that was some serious shit. Some scary shit.

Cass sighed, then stood. "You've got to be tired, Nix. Rest up. We'll figure out more tomorrow.

"Agreed." Del stood.

Everyone else followed, giving me hugs and filing out of the room. Only Ares didn't leave.

Instead, he stood by the door, as if uncertain. We were on a whole new ground here, I realized. Until now, he'd been the biggest threat in my life. Him and his Vampire Court. But now...

"You stayed by my bedside in the hospital," I said.

His brows rose, as if he didn't expect me to know that.

"Cass and Del told me."

"They ratted me out."

"They'll always rat you out." I grinned, and patted the couch next to me.

He approached and sat, not touching, but not on the farthest side either. He'd healed a lot faster than me, thanks to his vampire blood, and was looking damned good in his black sweater and jeans.

"How are you feeling?" Worry lines fanned out from his eyes.

"Great." I flexed my arm—the one that had been hanging weird after the explosion—and didn't even flinch.

"Good." His voice turned weary. "I was worried."

My heart warmed. The idea was...lovely. "When you jumped into the acid vines, you were choosing me over your court, weren't you?"

It was a bold statement, but it was also so obvious. And I needed to hear him say it. I'd been so wary of him for the whole of our weird relationship that I needed to look into his eyes when he said it.

"Yes." His voice didn't waver, his gaze was confident. "Yes. It was easy."

"So I can trust you?"

He nodded, the corner of his full lips curved up just slightly. "Yes. You can trust me. I'm on your team, Nix."

I smiled and shifted, leaning against him. He wrapped an arm around my shoulders. His heat and strength were delicious, sending a shiver through me that my exhausted body was too weak to act upon.

But I could still enjoy it.

Ares was on my side. As mandated by the goddesses of fate. But more importantly— by his own choice.

"We'll get this guy, Nix," Ares said. "Whatever he's up to— whatever that means for you and your role in the Triumvirate— we'll find him. And stop him."

"I hope so." The sheer enormity of what we could be facing made worry fizzle in my mind like soda. Cass and Del had faced some *enormous* challenges. World-changing challenges. And now, I had the first clue about mine.

"You've got a lot going for you," Ares said. "The Vampire Court as your allies, your hardcore friends—"

I chuckled. "They are pretty hardcore, aren't they?"

"Yes. I would not pick a fight with any of them."

I grinned.

"Or you," he said. "You're turning into one formidable supernatural."

"Not just a Conjurer anymore, huh? I've got all kinds of things I need to figure out."

"You've done a good job with the Destroyer magic."

"Trial by fire." I rubbed my stomach. "But I haven't felt queasy since the incident with the boat and the boulder. That really did teach me quick."

"You're a quick study. And you'll figure out this plant magic." He rubbed my shoulder and I leaned into his touch. "That is going to be a very powerful skill, I think."

I thought about my trove full of plants—of maybe showing it to him one day. Not yet. But soon, maybe. Because my new plant power made some sense when I thought about my trove. And the fact that I was supposed to be *Life.*

I snuggled deeper into Ares's shoulder, luxuriating in his warmth and strength. Because I'd had some of his blood to heal my post-explosion wounds, I was more in-tune than ever with his emotions. It was strange to feel what another felt. I didn't fool myself into thinking I felt *everything*.

But I could definitely sense the pure contentment that he felt just from sitting next to me. It was a bit weird, being here with the man I'd mistrusted since the moment he'd appeared at my door.

But I could trust him now. His actions, and his feelings, made that clear. And it was a good thing—for more than just my crazy libido.

I needed allies. All the allies I could get, if Laima was right about what I faced. The miserable women on the Vampire Court, my friends, Ares—whoever I could get.

"I think we can do this," I murmured.

"We can." He squeezed my shoulders.

I didn't know where all this was going. The thing with Ares, the mob boss, the beaker, the Triumvirate. But I wanted to find out. It was time. I'd waited long enough to fulfill my destiny. And fate was making it clear that I wouldn't have to wait much longer.

~~~

I hope you liked *Trial by Magic*! Want to find out how Del, Cass, & Nix escaped their evil ex-boss? Sign up for my mailing list to get the free novella *Hidden Magic*. There's also an excerpt up next.

THANK YOU FOR READING!

I hope you enjoyed reading this book as much as I enjoyed writing it. Reviews are *so* helpful to authors. I really appreciate all reviews, both positive and negative. If you want to leave one, you can do so at Amazon or GoodReads.

AUTHOR'S NOTE

Thank you so much for reading *Trial by Magic!* If you've read any of my other books, you won't be surprised to hear that I included historical and mythological elements. If you're interested in learning more about that, read on. At the end, I'll talk a bit about why Nix and her *deirfiúr* are treasure hunters and how I try to make that fit with archaeology's ethics (which don't condone treasure hunting, as I'm sure you might have guessed).

Now, onto the history and mythology in *Trial by Magic!* First —the mythology. The vampire realm shares cultural elements with the Baltic region. In Latvian folklore, a *Burtnieki* is a type of wizard. Originally, *Burtnieki* may have been practitioners of folk medicine. However, witch hunts in the 16th and 17th centuries led to a greater belief in evil spirits and magic users, which is how the *Burtnieki* may have made the jump from medical man to wizard.

Laimi, Dēkla , and Kārta were borrowed directly from Latvian mythology as well. They are the three fate goddesses, each with a slightly different role. They are sisters, though Laima is the most popular. She is the one who decides on the final fate of a person, so it is no surprise that people are most interested in her. Traditionally, Dēkla is associated with children and Kārta with adults. There was no reference to them being warriors, but it seemed like a fun addition to make to their story. Pūķis are also from mythology—they are Latvian dragons that are household spirits. They could protect the wealth of their owners and were also fed the first of every meal.

The artifacts that Nix and her *deirfiúr* preserve come from all different periods and cultures. I chose a beaker (a simple clay vase) from the Bell Beaker culture (2900 - 1800 BC in Europe) because it is simple and unassuming looking. Though there are many fabulous-looking artifacts, the plain ones have great value too. While it is fun to learn about the outliers—the biggest, most beautiful, most valuable, or the kings, queens, and nobility —the regular everyday objects can often tell us the most about how the majority people really lived. The simple beaker seemed like a good representative for that. You can read a bit more about the Bell Beaker culture in the Author's Note in *Fugitive of Magic*.

Though Cass and Nix returned the beaker to a cave in the Yorkshire Dales, there's no archaeological evidence suggesting that the Bell Beaker culture utilized the caves in this way. However, the caves are so interesting and such a great setting that I put the supernatural members of the Bell Beaker culture into those caves. The artifacts that Nix saw on the tables with the beakers would have been the most common types made by the Bell Beaker people. They were skilled metalworkers who specialized in copper, bronze, and gold and archaeological sites have revealed jewelry, daggers, and buttons.

Massive caves are all over the Yorkshire Dales, deep underground, and have a fascinating history of their own—particularly of early human exploration. Through my research, I learned that there are some really brave people out there, willing to crawl into tunnels and explore. Some of the names of the caves are really fun— the Molestrangler and Death's Head Hole. If you're interested in adventure stories and daring, I suggest giving the caves in the Yorkshire Dales a Google.

That's it for the historical influences in *Trial by Magic*. However, one of the most important things about this book is how Nix and her *deirfiúr* treat artifacts and their business, Ancient Magic.

As I'm sure you know, archaeology isn't quite like Indiana Jones (for which I'm both grateful and bitterly disappointed). Sure, it's exciting and full of travel. However, booby-traps are not as common as I expected. Total number of booby-traps I have encountered in my career: zero. Still hoping, though.

When I chose to write a series about archaeology and treasure hunting, I knew I had a careful line to tread. There is a big difference between these two activities. As much as I value artifacts, they are not treasure. Not even the gold artifacts. They are pieces of our history that contain valuable information, and as such, they belong to all of us. Every artifact that is excavated should be properly conserved and stored in a museum so that everyone can have access to our history. No one single person can own history, and I believe very strongly that individuals should not own artifacts. Treasure hunting is the pursuit of artifacts for personal gain.

So why did I make Nix and her *deirfiúr* treasure hunters? I'd have loved to call them archaeologists, but nothing about their work is like archaeology. Archaeology is a very laborious, painstaking process—and it certainly doesn't involve selling artifacts. That wouldn't work for the fast-paced, adventurous series that I had planned for *Dragon's Gift*. Not to mention the fact that dragons are famous for coveting treasure. Considering where the *deirfiúr* got their skills from, it just made sense to call them treasure hunters.

Even though I write urban fantasy, I strive for accuracy. The *deirfiúr* don't engage in archaeological practices—therefore, I cannot call them archaeologists. I also have a duty as an archaeologist to properly represent my field and our goals—namely, to protect and share history. Treasure hunting doesn't do this. One of the biggest battles that archaeology faces today is protecting cultural heritage from thieves.

I debated long and hard about not only what to call the heroines of this series, but also about how they would do their jobs. I wanted it to involve all the cool things we think about when we think about archaeology—namely, the Indiana Jones stuff, whether it's real or not. But I didn't know quite how to do that while still staying within the bounds of my own ethics. I can cut myself and other writers some slack because this is fiction, but I couldn't go too far into smash and grab treasure hunting.

I consulted some of my archaeology colleagues to get their take, which was immensely helpful. Wayne Lusardi, the State Maritime Archaeologist for Michigan, and Douglas Inglis and Veronica Morris, both archaeologists for Interactive Heritage, were immensely helpful with ideas. My biggest problem was figuring out how to have the heroines steal artifacts from tombs and then sell them and still sleep at night. Everything I've just said is pretty counter to this, right?

That's where the magic comes in. The heroines aren't after the artifacts themselves (they put them back where they found them, if you recall)—they're after the magic that the artifacts contain. They're more like magic hunters than treasure hunters. That solved a big part of my problem. At least they were putting the artifacts back. Though that's not proper archaeology, I could let it pass. At least it's clear that they believe they shouldn't keep the artifact or harm the site. But the SuperNerd in me said, "Well, that magic is part of the artifact's context. It's important to the artifact and shouldn't be removed and sold."

Now *that* was a problem. I couldn't escape my SuperNerd self, so I was in a real conundrum. Fortunately, that's where the immensely intelligent Wayne Lusardi came in. He suggested that the magic could have an expiration date. If the magic wasn't used before it decayed, it could cause huge problems. Think explosions and tornado spells run amok. It could ruin the entire site, not to mention possibly cause injury and death. That would be very bad.

So now you see why Nix and her *deirfiúr* don't just steal artifacts to sell them. Not only is selling the magic cooler, it's also better from an ethical standpoint, especially if the magic was going to cause problems in the long run. These aren't perfect solutions—the perfect solution would be sending in a team of archaeologists to carefully record the site and remove the dangerous magic—but that wouldn't be a very fun book.

Thanks again for reading (especially if you got this far!). I hope you enjoyed the story and will stick with Nix on the rest of her adventure!

GLOSSARY

Alpha Council - There are two governments that enforce law for supernaturals—the Alpha Council and the Order of the Magica. The Alpha Council governs all shifters. They work cooperatively with the Alpha Council when necessary—for example, when capturing FireSouls.

Blood Sorceress - A type of Magica who can create magic using blood.

Conjurer - A Magica who uses magic to create something from nothing. They cannot create magic, but if there is magic around them, they can put that magic into their conjuration.

Dark Magic - The kind that is meant to harm. It's not necessarily bad, but it often is.

Deirfiúr - Sisters in Irish.

Demons - Often employed to do evil. They live in various hells but can be released upon the earth if you know how to get to them and then get them out. If they are killed on Earth, they are sent back to their hell.

Dragon Sense - A FireSoul's ability to find treasure. It is an internal sense that pulls them toward what they seek. It is easiest to find gold, but they can find anything or anyone that is valued by someone.

Elemental Mage – A rare type of mage who can manipulate all of the elements.

Enchanted Artifacts – Artifacts can be imbued with magic that lasts after the death of the person who put the magic into the artifact (unlike a spell that has not been put into an artifact—these spells disappear after the Magica's death). But magic is not stable. After a period of time—hundreds or thousands of years depending on the circumstance—the magic will degrade. Eventually, it can go bad and cause many problems.

Fire Mage – A mage who can control fire.

FireSoul - A very rare type of Magica who shares a piece of the dragon's soul. They can locate treasure and steal the gifts (powers) of other supernaturals. With practice, they can manipulate the gifts they steal, becoming the strongest of that gift. They are despised and feared. If they are caught, they are thrown in the Prison of Magical Deviants.

The Great Peace - The most powerful piece of magic ever created. It hides magic from the eyes of humans.

Hearth Witch – A Magica who is versed in magic relating to hearth and home. They are often good at potions and protective spells and are also very perceptive when on their own turf.

Informa - A supernatural who can steal powers.

Magica - Any supernatural who has the power to create magic —witches, sorcerers, mages. All are governed by the Order of the Magica.

The Origin - The descendent of the original alpha shifter. They are the most powerful shifter and can turn into any species.

Order of the Magica - There are two governments that enforce law for supernaturals—the Alpha Council and the Order of the Magica. The Order of the Magica govern all Magica. They work cooperatively with the Alpha Council when necessary—for example, when capturing FireSouls.

Phantom - A type of supernatural that is similar to a ghost. They are incorporeal. They feed off the misery and pain of others, forcing them to relive their greatest nightmares and fears. They do not have a fully functioning mind like a human or supernatural. Rather, they are a shadow of their former selves. Half-bloods are extraordinarily rare.

Seeker - A type of supernatural who can find things. FireSouls often pass off their dragon sense as Seeker power.

Shifter - A supernatural who can turn into an animal. All are governed by the Alpha Council.

Transporter - A type of supernatural who can travel anywhere. Their power is limited and must regenerate after each use.

Vampire - Blood drinking supernaturals with great strength and speed who live in a separate realm.

Warden of the Underworld - A one of a kind position created by Roarke. He keeps order in the Underworld.

ABOUT LINSEY

Before becoming a writer, Linsey Hall was a nautical archaeologist who studied shipwrecks from Hawaii and the Yukon to the UK and the Mediterranean. She credits fantasy and historical romances with her love of history and her career as an archaeologist. After a decade of tromping around the globe in search of old bits of stuff that people left lying about, she settled down and started penning her own romance novels. Her Dragon's Gift series draws upon her love of history and the paranormal elements that she can't help but include.

COPYRIGHT